CHESTER CRICKET'S NEW HOME

YEARLING BOOKS are designed especially to entertain and enlighten young people. Patricia Reilly Giff, consultant to this series, received her bachelor's degree from Marymount College and a master's degree in history from St. John's University. She holds a Professional Diploma in Reading and a Doctorate of Humane Letters from Hofstra University. She was a teacher and reading consultant for many years, and is the author of numerous books for young readers.

GEORGE SELDEN

Chester Cricket's New Home

ILLUSTRATED BY

Garth Williams

A YEARLING BOOK

Published by
Bantam Doubleday Dell Books for Young Readers
a division of
Bantam Doubleday Dell Publishing Group, Inc.
1540 Broadway
New York, New York 10036

ISBN: 0-440-41246-3

Reprinted by arrangement with Farrar, Straus & Giroux, Inc.

Printed in the United States of America

October 1984

20   19   18   17   16   15

OPM

For Sarah, Beth, Mary, and Ben—
From a somewhat inattentive,
but genuinely loving uncle.

G.S.

CONTENTS

CHESTER CRICKET'S NEW HOME

ONE

Tragedy! With a Splash

Chester Cricket was feeling jumpy. And it wasn't the good kind of "jumpiness" that he often felt—when he hopped across the brook, for example, all the way from his stump to the mossy bank on the other side. He sometimes would make that flying leap just for the pure young fun of it. But not now. This was more a worrying, fidgeting feeling. In fact, Chester Cricket had a foreboding. He decided it really must be a foreboding—although, to be honest, he had to admit that he didn't quite know just what a foreboding was. But Simon Turtle had said that he had one a month ago, and that same afternoon—a lovely bright day in July it was—a storm had come up and a tall ash tree got struck by lightning. A mockingbird lost his home. (But he built a new one in Bill Squirrel's squirrel's elm.)

"A foreboding," said Chester gloomily, as he stared

3

out the hole of the stump where he lived. "That's what I've got all right."

It seemed a peculiar day to be gloomy. The rich light of a late August afternoon lay softly on the whole Old Meadow, now known as Tucker's Countryside. It had been renamed after Chester's friends Tucker Mouse and Harry Cat had saved it from destruction. And although all the folks who lived there referred to it now as Tucker's Countryside—or simply The Countryside—in their secret hearts all the animals round about, be they rabbit or turtle or cricket, still felt that it was the good, familiar Old Meadow. It was Chester's world—a world of grass, reeds, trees, of Tuffet Country and Pasture Land, with the brook running through it like a song running through your head when you're happy. And now it lay under a golden sun at the end of a flawless summer day that should have felt as full and ripe as a peach. But it didn't. It felt, well, nervous. The world felt nervous. At least to Chester Cricket it did.

"I just can't get enough of this place," said a lady's voice, behind Chester's stump.

A second lady sighed with pleasure. "Oh, neither can I, May! It's like a little paradise. I'd die without it. Gosh, I'm tired." The pleasure sighed off in a weary groan.

Tragedy! With a Splash

Chester recognized those ladies' voices. Ever since Tucker and Harry had rescued the Old Meadow by convincing the citizens of the town of Hedley that this was the site of the old Hedley homestead, the human beings had treated the place as if it were sacred. (Which suited the animals, birds, reptiles, insects, and fish who lived there very well indeed! They didn't get hunted, captured, exterminated, or even stepped on any more.) By order of the Town Council, many delightful winding paths had been laid out, so that people could meander beside the brook and beneath the trees, to enjoy the "unspoiled nature." But they had to stay strictly on the paths—a lot of disagreeable signs said so—in order not to spoil the charming wilderness.

One of these paths ran behind Chester's stump. Most stumps do not have a front or back, of course, but Chester's did, because the opening to his hole overlooked a little patch of grass that sloped down to the brook. That obviously, both Nature and Chester decided, was meant to be a front yard—with a water view. What made it especially nice was that Chester could sit in his front door, observing the gurgling foam beneath him, where the brook raced over a stretch of stones, without having any human beings poke their noses down to spy on him. Chester Cricket, like many insects and animals—and a few wise human beings—enjoyed his privacy.

But sometimes he liked to jump up on his stump and do a little spying himself. Human beings, from Chester's point of view—the top of his stump, or a twig in a bush—were quite fascinating, a curious study, although somewhat clumsy compared to a cricket. It had been up there, on his roof, that Chester became acquainted with the two ladies who were talking now. (He became acquainted with *them*, but they never so much as *noticed* him.)

They were Lola and May—he hadn't heard their last names—and they'd come every sunny day that summer to walk in Hedley's Meadow, which was what the human beings had renamed the Old Meadow, which was also Tucker's Countryside. As a matter of fact, for a few square miles of greenery it had more names than any comparable plot of land in all of Connecticut.

Their "constitutional" was how May and Lola referred to their daily walk. Although they were not old—indeed, they only referred to each other as "middle-aged" behind each other's back—they were far enough along to know that they needed some exercise. Especially since—and this they never referred to at all, behind or in front of anyone's back—they were both quite "stout." (Not even in their secret hearts would either of them use the dread word "fat.")

"I love this part of the meadow especially," said Lola, "but I wish they'd put more of those benches around here."

"Well, this is the wild part," said May. "They just let Nature go back to itself."

"Hmm," thought Chester inside his stump. He looked across the brook. "Wild Nature going back to itself" seemed to mean that at least here the human beings had left a few reckless weeds and a nervous sapling free to grow, without being trimmed back within an inch of their lives. Chester liked the fact that in this corner where the brook made its turn there weren't those dratted benches all over.

"My feet are just killing me!" Lola groaned.

Chester looked at all his feet and laughed. He had quite a few—to be precise, six—and he couldn't remember a single one of them ever being sore.

"There *is* that old stump—"

Chester Cricket stopped laughing.

"—You might be able to rest on that, dear."

"Aren't *you* tired, May?"

"As a matter of fact—"

"Come on, dear. It's broad enough for us both."

Chester wanted to warn—chirp—shout!—that his

7

stump was absolutely *not* broad enough for two over-weight ladies. He would have jumped up there himself, in hopes that the two ladies were afraid of insects, but if he did that, he realized, a terrible fate was sure to befall him—besit on him, in fact.

"I hope it won't smear us. It looks sort of wet."

"We've had so much rain this summer."

"Here goes—"

"*No!*" The cricket gave his loudest chirp.

Too late.

For the stump *was* soggy. And it was old. And worm-eaten too. (The worms didn't bother Chester at all. They kept to themselves. Worms *like* living in the woodwork, alone.) Indeed, Chester's very last thought, as the feeble, weakened walls of his home came crashing in around him, was actually for the worms. He hoped a few of them might survive—since he was certain that he would not—and he tried very hard to think of the worms, in order not to feel his fear. With a heavy *sqwunch* the stump collapsed. A big splinter of wood fell across Chester's back—he lay in the darkness, still as death.

"Good Lord!" came May's voice.

"Mercy!" said Lola.

There followed two very copious splashes: the ladies had slipped from the sagging stump and fallen in the

brook. And the squeaks, the squawks, and the spluttering that then arose would have made a whole flock of geese landing in a lake sound shy by comparison.

In the choppy and chaotic black it occurred to Chester that he could hear the women floundering in the water—a very good sign. He stretched a leg—he could feel as well, although he was pinned beneath the wood. With a surge and a silent chirp of joy he realized that he wasn't dead. Just trapped, he was, but badly trapped: he could only move three legs a little and couldn't shift his position at all.

Outside, the feminine commotion was moving up the bank as the ladies rolled and crawled from the brook. There were many "Land sakes!" and many "My stars!" and several "Oh, dears!" and one or two swearwords—polite ones, though—before Lola and May had righted themselves. The last thing Chester heard, as they squished away down the path to the road, was one asking the other if she thought the driver would let them on the bus— "in all these sopping clothes!" (He did. And to tell the truth, it was only a week or so before the whole accident became an adventure, and fun, for the ladies. Their "stump story" they called it, and told it and boasted and laughed about it for the rest of their lives.)

It was no fun for Chester, however. After testing his

six legs, he tried to move his antennae. There was no
space to wave them around, of course, but he could
feel them both, unbroken, which seemed like kind of
a miracle, they were so very long and delicate. One
wing ached badly—it was caught in an awkward position—and the other was tucked and trapped beneath
him. But that splinter of wood that held him fast had
saved his life. It was propped at an angle that kept him
from being completely crushed.

Tragedy! With a Splash

So, having discovered that he hadn't yet flown his last flight or chirped his last chirp, Chester Cricket wondered what to do. There was no point in trying to dig his way out. He was buried in stump, surrounded by stump, with at least a foot of crushed stump above him. The only thing to do was wait—and waiting, simply keeping still, especially when you can barely move, as anyone knows who's been forced to do it, is the hardest, most trying task of all. Impossible, even. Horrible! Chester wished he could chirp his shortest song. But his wings, which he used to make his music, were locked.

Was that a twitter from outside the stump?

"Hello!" Chester shouted. "Hey! Hel-*lo!*"

"That you, Chester Cricket?" asked a burbly voice. "John Robin—?"

"He's alive!" shouted John, and sang a sweet phrase out of sheer happiness. There seemed to be a little murmur of voices, a wave of relief, as if many other folk from the Meadow were gathered around outside the stump, in the rich gold light Chester couldn't see.

"Oh, John"—the cricket heaved a huge sigh of relief himself—"I'm so glad that—"

"Chester, you never will guess what happened!" said

John. "There were these two ladies—both plump as quail—and I guess they got tired, because they sat on your stump, and—"

"John—"

"—and then fell right smack into the brook! Can you beat that?"

"No, John, I can't beat that," said Chester Cricket, as patiently as he could. "But, John, I sort of was wondering—"

"The one in the red blouse went in head first!" John Robin went on merrily. He was one of Chester's really good friends, but being a robin, he was rather birdlike —flighty, in fact—and had a tendency to twitter. "Dorothy said—she was up in the nest—" Dorothy was John Robin's wife. They lived in the same nest together, in the willow tree beside Chester's stump. "—And she said that something like that—falling into the brook head first—could mess up a woman's hair badly."

"John!"

"But we did have a good laugh! Until we saw that the stump was smashed. And then we wondered—"

"John Robin! *Get me out of here!*"

"Oh," said John. And then he fell silent. The silence lasted. Too long. "How?"

"Well—well—can't you find a way, John? Who's out there, anyway?"

Tragedy! With a Splash

"Um—there's a gang of beetles"—Chester could almost feel John inspecting the crowd—"and a dragonfly. Oh, and Dorothy's here, too. She flew down. Say hello to Chester, Dorothy."

"Hello, Chester."

"Oh dear," Chester sighed. "Hello, Dorothy. If you both pecked together—"

"Not a chance," said John Robin jauntily. "That's a lot of stump you're inside of, Chester."

"I see," said Chester. "Well, in that case I'll just have to lie here patiently, with my aching wing, and wait until I starve to death, or suffocate, or the rest of the stump collapses on me and squashes me flat. Goodbye, everybody. John—Dorothy. You have all been grand! Give my love to the world."

There was some muffled but urgent talk outside the stump.

Then John said, "Chester, are you really very worried about being trapped in there?"

"Oh bug!" muttered Chester to himself. "That John sings a lovely song, he does—but he's one dumb robin!" Then right away he was mad at himself, for thinking that such a good friend was dumb. Aloud he said, "I am *very* worried, John! In fact, I can't begin to tell you how concerned I am."

"We'll think of something," said John.

Chester Cricket decided that if he waited for John to think, he might very well die of hunger—or old age. So he did a little quick thinking himself.

"John," he called, "is that dragonfly's name Donald?"

"Is your name Donald?"

"*Yiss!*" came a squeaky, raspy, thin voice.

"I know him," said Chester. "Donald, would you go ask Simon Turtle for help? Perhaps he can chew me out. Would you do that, please, Donald?"

"*Yiss!*"

There was a skittering of quick wings, which would have been inaudible to anyone who wasn't tuned, as Chester was, to insect things.

"I would have gone, Ches," John Robin said, and he sounded a little bit hurt.

"Oh no!" said Chester. "I want you to keep me company."

Simon Turtle had by far the strongest, sturdiest jaws in the Meadow. However, like John, he enjoyed conversation. And if the two of them got to talking, the day, the season, perhaps the year might very well have worn away, with Chester locked inside his stump like an insect frozen forever in stone. (When the cricket lived in New York one summer, he saw such a thing at the Museum of Natural History: an ant trapped in amber. It made him shiver.)

16

Tragedy! With a Splash

"Chester, are you still in there?" John called, after what seemed to both a very long moment. It seemed long to Chester because he was trapped, and to John because he'd gone almost a minute without saying a word.

"Oh, I'm still here," the cricket called back. "I won't make a move without letting you know."

To cheer his friend up, and pass the time, John told Chester all about how his son George—the youngest chick in his and Dorothy's latest batch—how George had flown all the way to East Puddum. That's the neighboring town, East Puddum is, next to Hedley. How George had flown to East Puddum last Wednesday just to test his wings—they were sound as two sails, too, just as sound as two sails! And then how his other son, James—he's the one who had his mother's markings—

"Can you see anybody yet?" chirped Chester plaintively.

"Well," said John, "that dragonfly's back."

"Donald? You there—?"

"*Yiss!*"

"Is Simon Turtle coming?"

"*Yiss!*"

Chester's wing was hurting more now, and the dark was getting on his nerves. It wasn't the free, starred dark of the night—it was close and cramped and dark, with only enough room left for worry.

He tried to rearrange his legs—just a little shift in position would help—and flexed an antenna, to prove he could. And he *did* wish that Simon Turtle would hurry. But turtles are slow, and Simon was old, and time dragged like an anchor.

TWO

Freedom—Finally!

Around the stump a soft murmur of insects, birds, and all the Meadow folk waiting there rose up like a bubble, excited, and burst.

"Hey, Chester—he's here!" John shouted.

The whole stump shivered a little as slow but methodical claws tugged a heavy weight up its broken side: Simon Turtle, inside his shell. "Got down as fast as I could, Chester." Puff! "Came down by brook instead of by bank"—puff!—"swimming and rolling most of the way. Thought that'd be quicker." Puff! Puff!

"Take it easy, Simon," Chester said. The good old turtle's raspy voice—not pretty but somehow reassuring, with all the unrushed wisdom of age—made the cricket feel almost safe already. "Rest now. Catch your breath. John Robin will tell you what happened."

"Don Dragonfly has already. Haven't you, Donald?"

"*Yiss!*"

The dragonfly could speak, if he wished—he once had told Chester about an encounter he had had with a bee—it's just that he was tight and private, the most private soul in the Meadow, in fact.

"I reckon the best place to start is where your front door is. Or was. *Was* this your front door, Chester?"

"I think so, Simon. My head is pointed toward your voice, and just before Lola and May sat down I remember looking out. If I'd been smart, I'd have jumped—brook or not."

"You keep talking now. You sound pretty close, and I wouldn't want to take your head off by mistake."

Working now with his claws and now with his formidable black jaws—they came together just like a vise—Simon Turtle started in to work.

"I was wondering," said Chester, "are you a snapping turtle, Simon? With those big jaws of yours?"

"No, I'm not," Simon answered. "I mean, naturally I've done some snapping in my time—all turtles have —but nothing professional, you might say."

The best way to clear the ruined stump, Simon found, was to bite off pieces of wood with his mouth, spit them out, and then brush them away with a claw. The old stump was soft and sticky and dead. It smelled

Freedom—Finally!

kind of stuffy and tasted queer. "Like a moldy sponge," Simon said.

"It's my home," said Chester ruefully. "Or it was."

After maybe the turtle's third or fourth rest: "Light!" exclaimed Chester. "I can see light!"

Simon took a fresh breath. "Be careful now. And hold still," he warned. "This is the tricky part."

Chester shut his eyes and held his breath as Simon's jaws crunched nearer and nearer. "If you'll just—my antennae—be extra special—I feel something—"

"I will be. I will be. There! Got one free. Can you move it?"

"Yes!" Chester raised and dipped, and then swung his antenna around in a circle. "Gosh! What a relief—!" The fresh air—so often it's taken for granted —felt like a silent, faithful friend.

In a minute the cricket's whole head was free. It stuck out of the stump like a little doorknob. He looked around— "Well, hello, everybody!"—and was shocked and a little embarrassed to see all the animals, insects, birds, one turtle, and everyone else who was gathered there. "One cricket, coming up," he said, and would have blushed, if a cricket could.

Apart from Donald, and John and Dorothy, there was Hank Blue Jay, and Beatrice Pheasant, a rabbit

named Robert who got indignant if anyone called him Bob—although most animals wanted to, since Robert Rabbit was hard to say—and quite a few others, too. Emily Chipmunk, a fretful soul, was just hurrying up, saying, "My! my! my! This is awful! Oh dear! This is really awful! Chester—are you all right?"

"I'm fine." He was free to his first set of shoulders now. "You calm down, Emily."

It seems that word of Chester's predicament had

spread through the Old Meadow like wildfire—the dreaded wildfire which all Meadow dwellers feared. Chester Cricket, despite his size and apart from his fame in New York, was something of a favorite. People looked up to him—or down to him, as the case might be—and respected his judgment. So when news of his danger was whispered through the grass, the trees, or sung through the open air, all gathered to see if they could help—and also, since beasts and people are like that, just out of curiosity.

With a rather grand flourish—a little grander than need be, in fact, but this was his largest audience since he had chirped his songs in New York—Chester Cricket jumped from his imprisonment to the patch of grass beside the brook. "Da *daa!*" he couldn't keep himself from singing, as he flew through the air—but then couldn't keep himself from tripping as he landed off-balance and tumbled into the water himself. "Just like Lola and May," he laughed, as he scrambled out. "And serves me right for showing off."

For a minute or two, as Chester accepted congratulations from all his friends on still being alive, he didn't look back at the stump. When he did—"Oh, my *gosh!*"—it teetered above him in much worse condition than

he'd ever imagined. One whole side was gone completely. That was where May had sat—the heftier of the two. And the other was a shambles of twisted, broken wood. There was no nice flat top left at all—not even a space for a cricket to perch. It was late in the afternoon by now, and even the sunlight, gold as it was, and sloping in from the radiant west, seemed melancholy at such a sight.

No one spoke. Then Simon Turtle said, "Well, Chester, I guess you'll have to move."

"*Move*—?" The thought struck the cricket as if some stranger had flicked an antenna. "I don't want to move! I've lived in that stump all my life."

"Can't see how you'll live there now." Simon slowly shook his withered, wise head. "Not safe. And pretty messy, too."

"But *moving*—" The idea got bigger and bigger. It felt like a weight on Chester's back, much worse than when he'd been trapped in the stump.

Simon tried to help. "Well, most folks have to move, Chester—sometime."

"When did *you* move last, may I ask?"

"Oh, I never move. I've lived in my pool, beside my log, for longer than stones."

"See!"

"I move every year," John Robin offered. "I build

a new nest—new twigs, new pieces of string and things —all new furniture, every year!"

"I want my old stump back," said the cricket despondently.

"You're not going to get it, Chester, my lad," said Simon Turtle, stern but soft.

Right there, beside his brook, and bathed in a puddle of sun, surrounded by most of his friends in the world, Chester Cricket felt more alone than he ever had in his life. More even than on that day in the Times Square subway station when he found himself hiding in a pile of rubbish. He felt downright desolate.

"Well," he said, "I can always go back to New York. I'm sure Tucker and Harry will take me in."

A chorus of *"No's!"* rose into the air. Consternation buzzed in this ordinarily quiet corner of the Old Meadow. Wings, whiskers, antennae—whatever it was that the animals had, to show deepest feelings—everything wiggled nervously at the thought of Chester Cricket leaving.

John Robin chirruped impetuously, "Why, Dorothy and I would *love* to have you—"

And Emily Chipmunk squeaked her idea: "There's *plenty* of space! Now that Henry's away at Ellen's house."

Even Beatrice Pheasant burbled politely, in her most

cultivated tone of voice: "Jerome and I live under some most attractive tuffets, Chester. Oodles of room! On the other side."

"Do you want to go back to New York?" asked Simon.

"No," said Chester. "I did that once. New York just never felt like home. But *this*"—this was all his cricket's eyes could see: trees, reeds, low shrubs, the August flowers—a world—"this does."

"Then it's settled," said Simon. "We'll find a place. For now, you better come home with me. There's a crack in my log you can stay in tonight."

"Well"—Chester took one last, dejected look at his stump—"all right."

"Come along, then. Have to go by bank. I can't swim upstream. Maybe once, when I was younger, but—"

"My bell! My bell's still in there!" Home might be destroyed—but one thing at least must not be lost, so the past wouldn't be forgotten completely.

"What bell?" said Simon.

"It came from New York—from way downtown—from Chinatown!—and Sai Fong gave it to Mario and Mario said it was mine—and it *is*! I brought it all the way from New York. And I won't budge a jump without it!"

"Well, land!" said the turtle. "If it means that

much—!" He lumbered and waddled up on his four legs, hauling his heavy shell along, and began scratching at the ruins of stump, near the place where Chester had been pinned down. "Mm, let me see—" A few private mumbles helped him to work. "—No bell here, none that I can see. My goodness, what a mess!"

A little muffled clink came from the dead center of the stump.

"That sounds like it!" called Chester from below.

"I b'lieve it is."

"Try not to dent it, Simon—please."

"I won't dent it if—drat!" There was more mumbling, and then some fussing—Simon seemed to be trying to push something out of his mouth with a claw —and then what sounded suspiciously to Chester like spitting. "Simon," he called, "did you swallow it?"

" 'O!" Very slowly the turtle came backwards down from the stump, with his rear legs feeling a safe way behind. "I 'ot it 'uck on 'y 'aw! 'Et it off!"

The hook of the little bell was caught on the inner corner of Simon Turtle's lower jaw. Chester gently reached in and pried it off. "My very own bell! No bigger than a honeybee." He held it up and shook: *pling! pling!* "And it's safe! Undented."

Although the bell was very heavy—after all, a grown-up honeybee is at least half as big as a cricket—

in two hops Chester had it at the edge of the brook, where he washed off little chips of wood. "If my bell survives, then so can I!" In his secret heart Chester Cricket had always believed—at least he had hoped—that his chirps sounded sort of like his bell.

"Come on," said Simon. "It's 'most dark now. We've got to be getting back to my log."

Chester thanked everybody for worrying and coming to help him. "And thank you especially, Donald," he said. "It was good of you to get Simon."

"*Yiss!*"

In the last ray of afternoon light the elegant wings

of the dragonfly dripped myriad colors—green, gold, blue, ruby red, and silver—as if a whole rainbow had formed a single drop on Donald. He hovered a moment, motionless, miraculously still in the air. Then dashed away—vanished. Evening fell on the Meadow.

THREE

Simon's Log

A ripening moon that was swelling toward the full
shone down on Chester and Simon as they made their
slow way through Tuffett Country and Pasture Land.
The cricket was hopping heavily because of the bell
he was carrying with his first two legs, and Simon
Turtle was never one for hurrying. On one side of
them were the tall reeds, barely silvery green in the
dark, that grew beside the brook, and on the other the
land stretched away, past shrubs and stretches of open
grass—the kind of delicious meadow grass that cows
had browsed on long ago when farmers pastured their
herds there. Beyond low hills there was the road—the
lights of cars were flashing along it—and past the road
the houses began. The Meadow always felt to Chester
—and never more so than on this night, with the
sound of running water beside him—like a wet rich

refuge where things could grow, surrounded by the dry town outside.

They forded the brook a little way before Simon's Pool. Luckily, there were two stepping-stones—set there for the human visitors. Otherwise, with that bell of his, Chester couldn't have made it in one jump.

"There she be," said Simon, nodding up. "My log." From the comfortable tone in his voice Chester knew he meant *my home.*

Actually, Simon's "home" was more of an estate than one certain special place, like Chester's stump. He spent just as much time down in his pool, where he had a comfortable pebble bed, or up on the bank, as he did on his log. But somehow, when Meadow folk thought of Simon, they always pictured him up on his log, remembering something from times gone by or lecturing one of the younger beasties—a baby rabbit, say—on how a task should be properly done—say, eating clover: not too close to the ground—it won't grow back.

"Hop up there, Chester. Crack's on top, so you'll see the sky, but facing poolside, for a nice earth view."

Chester got on the log with one big jump, still hugging his bell, and then inched forward, toward where it lifted into the night.

"You find it?"

"Yes. It's pretty small."

"Can you fit in?"

"I guess so. Barely."

There was just enough room for the cricket to tuck his bell in the crack—the bell seemed much larger now—but that didn't leave enough space for Chester.

Simon Turtle called up, "You all snugged down for the night?"

"Oh, I'm snugged, all right!" said Chester. "My head's inside my bell. That's the only way I can stretch out."

"You don't say!" remarked Simon, with philosophical interest. "I don't doubt you're the very first cricket to do that."

"I don't doubt it, either. Good—"

Chester never said "—night."

For from Simon's Pool, in a raucous, wheezy, madcap voice—some might have said that it sounded crazy —there rose this song: "*Ohhhh—*

> *A cricket lived in a rickety stump—*
> *In a rickety stump lived he.*
> *But May and Lola sat down—**Whump!***
> *Said cricket, "Woe is me!"*

"What on earth—?" began Chester.

But Simon was laughing. "I hear you, Walt!"

"He! he! har! har! and ho! ho!" came the voice.

"Now stop that, Walt! Go to sleep. Chester's had a tumultuous day. So've I. You let us rest."

"Okay." There was a quick little swish in the darkness—by no means a plop—as if someone clever had ducked under the water.

"Who *is* that?" said Chester. "A fish?"

"You get to bed, too," Simon Turtle advised. His voice got suddenly small, far away, as only a turtle's voice can get when he pulls back his head in his shell. "Tomorrow morning you'll know all."

But next morning, when the sun in his eyes woke him up, Chester Cricket at first knew nothing—not even where he was. He found out soon enough, by bumping his head, with a very dull *thunk,* on the inside of his bell. That brought it all back. He found out that he had a stiff neck, too, from the awkward position in which he'd slept, with his head resting on the clapper. He craned up to look.

The crack in Simon's log faced southeast—a nice direction, despite the sun, for there across the sparkling pool the low part of the Meadow, dewy and fresh, was glistening under an August dawn. It shone as if Nature were made of wet gems.

Chester hopped to the highest part of the log. To one side, a little way back, there was kind of a mysterious place, a section of the Meadow that Chester didn't know too well. A spring rose there and formed a small trickle that fed the brook through the pool. And that trickle was snaky and strange. Queer weeds were waving like hair, back and forth, very slowly back and forth, beneath the water. The earth was damp and fertile and full. Unusual flowers and reeds covered it. There were lots of hidden things living there. Chester looked at that place. In its difference it seemed sort of scary and wonderful. He gave it a name: the Mystic Marsh.

"Good mornin'!" a voice behind him sang, in kind of an up-and-down melody—the same voice that Chester had heard last night.

He hopped around, and there in the pool he saw two eyes. There was something perplexing about those eyes, apart from the fact that they were almost submerged. Chester couldn't think what—but then he knew: those eyes looked like a magician's eyes: hypnotic, strange—and wonderful! Unnerving, they were. Chester realized that he hadn't even said "Hello."

"Hello!" The eyes disappeared—then a whole snake's head popped out of the water, just up to the neck. (The neck of a snake starts behind the head, but only the snake knows where it stops.)

"Morning, Walt." Simon Turtle was crawling methodically up his log. He'd slept pool-bottom, as he always called it, but now he was out to check on the weather. He usually took a few minutes each morning, testing the breeze, observing the sun or gauging the strength of the rain on his shell—giving the day his permission, you might say. It took him a long time to get next to Chester. "You know Walt yet, Chester?"

"No, I don't."

"Walter Water Snake—Chester Cricket." He coughed importantly. (Introductions can do that, sometimes: make people and animals feel important.) "Chester—Walt."

Now, Chester Cricket would have to admit that snakes were not his favorite folk. They had a reputation for eating insects. The only snake that Chester knew well—not well, you never could say they were really friends, but they had a working relationship— was a big, fat black snake named Frank. Their relationship worked largely because whenever Frank Black Snake looked hungry, Chester Cricket stayed out of his way. Other times they were cordial with one another, and always remained on speaking terms. But still . . . snakes . . .

"How-dee-do!" chortled Walter.

"Oh—I'm fine," replied Chester, and thought to himself that Walter Water Snake didn't seem much like his old acquaintance Frank at all. He wasn't big, and he wasn't fat—rather trim and sleek, in fact. And he was sort of—Chester searched for a word, and "goofy" was all that came to mind. "That is," he went on, "if you think anybody is fine who just had his house sat out of existence."

"I heard all about it! *Whump! Sqwush!*"

"Who told you?" Chester asked.

"*Guiss!*"

"Oh."

"That dragonfly was all over the Meadow while you and Simon the Swift were toddling home. Didn't say much, though. 'Chister's stump got squished!' was all. Then he lit out like greased lightning to bring the bulletin to a family of frogs. Good gossip it is, too! I have to admit. The bulrushes all alive with it!"

"Mmm!" muttered Chester, who was having mixed feelings about this snake. (Mixed feelings are those that you can't quite sort out. Some feel good, others don't.) For one thing, he thought it was rather impertinent to refer to the oldest Meadow dweller as "Simon the Swift," especially since even the mosquitoes knew that the venerable turtle was the slowest soul in the world. For another, "good gossip," he thought, was hardly a sympathetic description of his own catastrophe.

"Hey! How did you like my song last night?" Walt's head bobbed up and down in the water, like a cork expecting a compliment. " 'A cricket lived in a rickety stump—' "

"Oh, very nice." Chester fudged a bit.

"Say, in New York they never called you 'crickety,' did they?"

"No. Mama Bellini said 'cricketer' sometimes."

"Too bad," said Walter. "I could have composed, 'A crickety lives in a rickety'—et cetera. Crickety-rickety. Nifty rhyme! Get it?" His head ducked down—then out it popped. "Get it?"

"I get it," said Chester without too much enthusiasm.

"You and I could make sweet music, Chirpy Chester! I like to do words, and you make up the tunes. How about that?"

"I'll have to think," said Chester Cricket, but he didn't plan to think too long.

"You think then. Think!" Walter disappeared.

"Is he *always* like this?" said Chester to Simon.

"Most always." The turtle laughed. He didn't seem

to mind Walter Water Snake at all. "He's zany, isn't he?"

"I don't think I know what that means," said Chester.

"You stick around Walt long enough," said Simon, "you'll learn."

"I can't even tell if he's looking at me. His eyes go—"

"Did you think?" A familiar head flashed up so close that it almost toppled Chester over.

A turtle's chuckle is wonderful. Simon got one in his voice, and coughed to keep the laughter down. "Walt, Chester was saying while you were away, he can hardly tell which way you're looking—"

"Snake eyes!" Walter reared out of the water—at least his upper half. "I got the snake eyes, Chester—you bet! The authentic item—that's me! Have a look—" He stared at the cricket in a highly unsettling manner.

"Oo! Oh!" Chester blinked. "I wish you wouldn't do that, Walter. It's very disturbing. And dangerous for the eyes, as well."

"And not all snakes have the true and magic snake eyes." Walter flipped some water with his tail. "Now, there's a good friend of mine—a copperhead named Charleton—and, Cricket, Charleton C. has eyes like a little lamb—the darlin'! But he lacks snake eyes. Lives

up the brook a piece, he does—and happy as a dandelion."

Walter whacked the surface of the pool—just for fun. "You want to hear how I knew I had snake eyes, Chester C.?"

"Not really," said Chester. "For a cricket it is somewhat worrying—"

"I was out in the Meadow one afternoon, just sopping up sun for the fun of it, and this hoity-toity girl come along, with her boyfriend. They shouldn't have been in our lovely, enchanted Old Meadow at all! They should have been in a roller disco! His name was Billy! Billy Sweetie, she called him."

"What was *her* name?" said Chester. Despite his worries—stiff neck, no home—the cricket was starting to like this story. Walter Water Snake, he decided, was quite a raconteur. (That word means someone who tells stories well. Once in New York the cricket had heard his friend Harry Cat describe an old acquaintance of his—an owl who lived in the church of Saint Mark's in the Bowery—as a marvelous raconteur.)

"Her name was Toots," said Walter. "Or Tootsie. Billy called her both. She had shoes with high heels! Can you beat that, Crickety Chester—huh? Spiky heels! —to go strolling in the Meadow. Some people! And the clothes she was wearing! Yellow and purple slacks, and a blouse that started out to be green and ended up pink. It looked like ten different kinds of parrots had landed all over her. *And*—ooo, this made me mad!—a belt which suspiciously seemed to me as if it was made of snakeskin!"

"Oh boy," sighed Chester. He glanced at Simon, to share his sympathy, but found that the turtle was snickering.

"Come to think of it now, Miss Ditsy may have been somewhat nutty on the subject of snakes." Walt undulated his back in the water. He had a long back to undulate, too. "She had sequins all over that tacky colored blouse of hers. And sequins are just about as close as a human being can get to scales. Anyway"— he flipped himself out like a piece of rope—" I thought I would teach Tootsie Ditsy a lesson."

"Hee! hee!" Simon Turtle was wheezing in anticipation.

"I reared straight up! And although I'm no cobra, Chester ol' pal, I can rear pretty well—"

"So I see!"

"—and I gave her the old snake eyes!" Walt's head swung high, and then low, over Chester. Then he lounged back in the water comfortably, like someone in a rocking chair. "Well, let me tell you that that girl screamed—she said, '*Eek!*' "

"I heard it all the way here!" said Simon enthusiastically.

"'*Eek!*' she screamed. 'Oh, Billy, *eek!* There's a snake!' And, Chester, the two of them took off like a couple of broken dolls! The last I saw, they were falling all over a bunch of tuffets, scrambling toward the road. So *that* is how I know I've got the genuine snake eyes!" He finished his narrative happily, and poised before Chester. "Terrific—huh?"

"Oh, very good," Chester had to admit.

"Some might say cockeyed," Simon puffed through his chuckles.

But Chester, inside himself, sighed. And decided— "Good friends are wherever you're lucky enough to find them."

FOUR

John Robin and Friends

The morning had made up its mind by now: it was going to be hot. These last days of August sometimes were the sultriest ones of all. The summer seemed to have saved its strength, and then—perhaps warned by a single bright, cool day like September—in one week it burned up all its stored heat. A good time for insects, this time of year was. Chester Cricket and all his friends and relatives—cicadas, locusts, katydids—made music in the fields.

With his special liquid melody—all birds have their own, like signatures—John Robin coasted down through the air and alighted next to Chester. "Hi!"

"Hi, John."

"Nice day!"

"Yes, very."

Walter Water Snake raised two eyes suspiciously above the surface of Simon's Pool.

To show how nice and share his pleasure, John

sang his song a few more times. But, unlike every other day, his wordless tune brought no joy this morning to Chester Cricket. It hurt him, somehow. Ordinarily, hearing John pour forth his robin's throaty happiness —even show off a little, if he felt extra well—was one of Chester's greatest pleasures. Not now. It reminded him of all that had happened yesterday: that he had no place he could stand and say, "This is mine, my home, this is where I live."

"Hey, Chester—" John hopped from one foot to the other: a very good sign (among robins, that is)—"I've got good news! Your house—"

"My *stump*—?" hoped Chester, for a moment.

"Oh no. That's gone. Worse even today than last night. What's left of it's all falling down of its own accord."

No hope. "Oh."

"Better even!" the robin boasted. "We cleaned out an old squirrel's nest! My Dorothy and I, and whatever kids we could still collect—Jeanette and Joe volunteered—we spent half the night, oh, airing, and dusting, and shaking leaves out—"

"I am *not* going to live in one of Bill Squirrel's nests," said Chester firmly.

"Not Bill. You know Bill lives up there in the elm tree." With a flick of his wing John gestured toward a hill that rose above Simon's Pool. It was crowned by a soaring, splendid elm. Bill Squirrel had made his nest there for years. In fact, as John and Chester, and Simon and Walt, looked up, they saw a flash of gray in the leaves—which would have been a whisk of Bill, or else a patch of morning sky. "This is down at my willow," John went on. "Last summer, or maybe two summers ago—it could have been three—there was this squirrel, whose name was Lou—or was it Luke?—anyway, he built his nest in my willow tree."

"So this nifty nest is going on four years old?" asked Walt. He sank his head down so that only his eyes were staring gloomily over the water. His expression seemed even more skeptical because of one eye that headed toward the north.

"I think it's only two," said John Robin reassuringly. "Well—this Lou, or Luke, only stayed one year. He said he was restless, and never would take more than one summer in any particular meadow. Footloose is how he described himself."

"A bum, in fact," commented Walt. "At best a hobo."

"Oh, I wouldn't say that. He just had the itch to travel, that's all. So he put up this thing in my willow tree—"

"Har-har! he-he! and ho-ho!"

John Robin looked blank. Somebody unkind would have said he looked dumb—or at least dumbfounded. "Walt—what are you laughing at?"

"Nothing, Friendly Feathers—nothing. Come on—tell us more about Footloose Lou and his flimsy folly, soon to be known as Chester's Rest, or Cricket's Crack-up, as the case may be."

John looked at Chester; his eyes were glazed, as if an acorn had dropped on his head.

"Don't mind him, John," the cricket advised. "What else should I know? About this construction."

"Well, I'll admit," John Robin nodded, agreeing with himself, "it isn't exactly like one of Bill's nests. When Bill makes a nest, he makes it to last. But honestly, Chester, I think you'll like it. Dorothy and I were up half the night, patching with twigs all the holes that you might fall through. And the view is really beautiful! It isn't as high as me, of course, but you see the whole Meadow, and the brook down below, with your mashed-up old stump."

"The heart swells at the thought," said Walt. "A shack in the sky, overlooking a former home now squashed into ruins."

"Please come!" John urged. "I'll be a good neighbor. Honest I will."

"I'm sure you will, John." Chester shifted from one set of legs to the other. "It's just that—it's just—"

"Just what?" The robin seemed puzzled, and maybe a bit hurt.

Chester sighed. "I guess I have to move somewhere—"

"Come on!" John bobbed up and down beside him. He was all eagerness, if Chester was not. "Let's go right away! I'm dying to show you everything. And the folks are waiting."

"What folks?"

"Just *come on,* Chester! You'll see. You want me to carry your bell? I will—"

"I think I'll leave it here," said Chester. "Temporarily."

"Okay then. Grab on. I'll fly us over."

"I can fly," the cricket announced, "when I want to. Don't rush me. Anyway, I'd rather hop."

"We'll hop," said John obligingly.

"Hippety-hop to the willow top! Crickety-crack! There and back!" Walter Water Snake sang gaily, and blew bubbles in the pool.

"You're in a good mood today," said John.

"Always! Always!" Walter declared. "My one and only lovable failing."

"I'm beginning to know what 'zany' means," said Chester to Simon.

"Thought you might," the turtle replied.

"My only regret"—Walt loomed from the water, but didn't seem all that sad to Chester—"is that Cricket and I won't make music together. However"—he vanished—*whssh!*—and then reappeared—"someday we may."

"Come on!" John Robin urged again.

With one jump Chester cleared the pool and landed neatly on the bank. "Bye, Simon. Bye, Walter."

"Bye, Chester," the turtle called.

But Walter would have nothing at all to do with a farewell as simple as saying "Goodbye." He surfed to where the cricket was standing uncertainly and gave him a wink of his snake eyes. "Your antennae are drooping, Chester friend. Be not so sad! All may yet be well. Take care of him, Friendly Feathers! He! he! ho! ho!"

"—and har! har!" Chester Cricket finished it for him, none too happily, as he hopped away with John.

And next morning—"Ho! *ho!* What *is* this I see?" Walter sang his old refrain again, for there on the bank, in exactly the same place he'd been yesterday,

50

sat Chester Cricket. "It can't be that well-known home-owner—stump-jumper—"

"Oh, stop it!" said Chester. "I don't feel like joking."

"What happened?" said Walter. He lowered his head so it rested on the pool's smooth surface as if it were only a blue silk cushion, just put there for Walt to lean on and listen.

"Do you know what a housewarming is?" asked the cricket sadly.

"Can't say that I do. We had a little fire once, two tuffets down from the one where I often take the sun. Some idiot with a cigarette! But a bullfrog splashed water up from the brook. What *is* a housewarming?"

"A housewarming," began Chester, "I now know for sure, is a special party for someone who moves. His friends all get together and fix up his new home as nice as they can, and then they throw this enormous party, to mess it all up again."

"I see."

"And, Walter—" Chester sighed and shook his head, but decided he'd better get everything straight. "Now, I like birds, Walter. I really do. Relationships between birds and insects aren't always too great, but honestly, I do like birds."

"I take it that most of these housewarming party-goers were birds," said Walter.

"You wouldn't believe it! When me and Friendly Feathers—I mean, John Robin and I—"

Chester's story—he really was getting the feel of it now, and it felt kind of laughable—was interrupted right at the beginning by an old and creaky laugh, like a door on a squeaky hinge. Simon Turtle, who'd crawled up onto his log where it dipped in the water, had settled in to enjoy himself. "Go on," he encouraged. "Don't mind me. I just didn't want to miss the fun."

"Fun," Chester echoed. "Well—come to think—from all the jabber and bills clattering I guess everybody enjoyed themselves. Except me. But I was only the guest of honor. Anyway"—he took a storytelling breath—"John and I hopped down to the willow tree, and John flew me up to Lou's Lofty Lookout. That's what I decided to call it. Of course I could have jumped up myself, from branch to branch—I'd have had to learn, if that was going to be my home—but I thought this first day I might as well go up on the robin elevator. And I was tired. So much has happened these past two days—I just wanted to rest, and get my bearings."

"So how's the location?" asked Walt. "As spectacular as Friendly Feathers said?"

"It really is, but, you know, crickets are really earth types—stumps, logs—"

"Fireplaces—"

"Yes. But not so much for heights. And Lou's nest is *high!* At least on the tenth branch up. And it does overlook the whole Meadow, since it's built way out at the end. In fact"—Chester twitched an antenna—"a little too near the end. It made me feel woozy."

"You have acrophobia, Chester ol' pal?"

"I didn't think so till yesterday, Walt. In New York, Lulu Pigeon took me up to the top of the Empire State Building. Of course I fell *off!*—that's enough to give anyone fear of heights. But it wasn't so much it was high, Lou's nest, it's that it *swayed.* Back and forth, back and forth—*ooo-ah! ooo-ah!*—I got downright queasy. And there wasn't that much of a wind yesterday. Also"—Chester wrinkled his face in a grimace—"I may have gotten a little seasick because it still did smell of squirrel."

"I see." Walter did an S-curve in the pool. "Are there any other charms of this place you've neglected to tell us?"

"Not really. John and Dorothy had mended most of the holes. There *was* one rather big one left. But if I'd fallen out any time, I'd have had something soft to land

on. The nest is so far out on the branch that it overhangs the brook. Kind of shivery, in fact, to look through that hole and see the current swirling beneath."

"Umhmm," said Walter. "So the truth is, if you had fallen asleep one night—rocked seasick in the cradle of air—you might very well have dropped through a hole and fallen ten branches or more into the water."

"Yes, more or less," agreed Chester.

"Please proceed," Walt invited, in a silky, sly voice.

"Anyway, I didn't have very much chance to be sick. Because right away my life got almost scared out of me. I was only just starting to look over the nest—"

"Picking your way among the potholes," Walter put in.

"—when from everywhere there came this tremendous shout: SURPRISE! It's a good thing a squirrel's nest is all safe and snug. I'd have been blown clear out otherwise."

"A surprise party!" Walt frolicked around in the water. "But I thought it was a housewarming party."

"It was a combination surprise, housewarming, welcome-in and bring-a-little-something-you-don't-really-want-as-a-gift party. And, Walter, you cannot *imagine* how many birds crashed that party! That whole willow tree was just crawling with birds. They'd been hiding—behind leaves, under branches—just everywhere! Even some in a neighboring maple. And birds are very good, I've found, at not being seen when they don't want to be. But how they kept quiet I never will know. They made up for it later, that's for sure!"

"Take it from the big 'SURPRISE!' " said Walter Water Snake.

" 'Surprise!' they all shouted, and started piling into that nest and out along that branch. Within two minutes there were jillions of birds lined up. I thought, she's going to snap for sure. But she didn't. She held. I guess willow trees are used to birds' shenanigans. So anyway, Walt, there I was—"

"Birds to the right of you! Birds to the left of you! Birds above, and birds below!"

"It was utter pandemonium! And Dorothy Robin kept dashing up, saying, 'Chester dear, more company! More company, Chester!' She was the hostess, more or less."

"Dorothy always liked being hostess," Simon Turtle wheezed.

"A model of self-control, I've no doubt." Walter flipped his tail over his heart: a picture of innocence.

"Self-control! I thought to myself, if I don't fall out of this nest, she will. Walt"—a different little thought struck Chester—"are you making fun of me?"

"Wouldn't *dream* of it!" said the water snake. "But what about the things they brought? Little gifties, I presume. Come on, Creaky Cricket—tell me! Tell me! Tell me!"

Chester looked at Walter Water Snake quizzically; his eyes were asking him what he meant. He decided that even if Walter was making fun, it wasn't mean fun he was making. And also Chester—who'd been quite a star performer once—was rather enjoying Walter's rapt attention. With his grinning head poked up out of the water, the snake was an avid listener.

"The 'gifties' mostly were little things I was meant to enjoy in my new home," Chester went on. "But, actually, in a lot of cases I think it was stuff that the birds didn't want, or else they'd outgrown. I mean literally outgrown. Quite a few were molting, and they'd brought me a few of their own old feathers that should have been thrown away. 'For nesting,' they said. Well, Walt, *I* don't nest! Insects don't nest— except wasps and bees and others like them. If you call a hive a nest. And if I did, I wouldn't want to make my nest out of smelly old feathers and pieces of Kleenex and burlap scrounged up from heaven knows where."

"Didn't anyone bring food?" Walter asked.

"Oh, plenty! At least two dozen did! Lovely nuts, and berries, and a few choice seeds, and some even brought *worms!!*"

"A robin's delight," sighed Walt.

"And within five minutes the ones who'd brought the tastiest things had eaten them up, congratulating each other—and me—on how delicious everything was!"

Without a word, as fast as a breeze that wrinkles the surface, Walter flashed away, to the other end of

Simon's Pool, where he did some shaking and spluttering.

"And, Simon," said Chester, while Walt was gone, "the noise they made! You wouldn't be-*lieve*—"

"Wait! Wait!" Walter was back. "I don't want to miss a single word!"

"I was telling Simon about the racket."

"That's just birds, Chester," Simon said. "They love to get together and flock, and talk and flap and have a party."

"Well, they had a party, all right!" said the cricket. "That Dorothy Robin kept fluttering up, saying, 'Company's coming!' 'More company's coming!' 'Chester, here's some more company!' It got so the sound of that word—'company!'—would make my blood run cold. And then she'd reel off a string of names—none of which I'd remember. Except for Sam." Chester tightened his mouth, as if something didn't taste too good.

"Sam?" said Simon and Walter together. "Who's Sam?"

"Sam Grackle. He flew in about five o'clock."

"Five o'clock?" Walter Water Snake reared up—up —and then back, and hung suspended, incredulous, in the air. "How long did this party go on?"

John Robin and Friends

"*All day!* There were birds dropping in the whole afternoon! Every friendly feather in the township of Hedley—in all of Connecticut!—must have shown up. That's one more thing I found out about birds: the word spreads fast! Especially if there's a party involved."

Walter bobbed impatiently, prompting Chester. "So big Sam Grackle arrived when the festivities were well under way?"

"How do you know he was big?" said Chester.

"All grackles are big"—Walter whipped himself out impatiently, and then folded himself back into an S—"and a lot of them are stupid, too. Boors! Grackles are boors."

"That's Sam exactly. Big, stupid, and raucous. Was he noisy! 'Hi, gang!' he croaked, as he landed right on top of me. I was out on the branch by now—the nest was too crowded—and Big Sam came smashing right down on my back. He apologized, though. 'Didn't see you, kid. Ya're kinda little. Har! har!' And, Walt— when *you* say 'har! har!' I know it's a joke. You sort of say it to make fun of yourself. But when Big Sam Grackle said 'har! har!' he really meant *'har! har!'* That's just how he laughed. With a beak full of seed. You should have seen how he ate! He tore into those berries and nuts as if there were famine dead ahead. And all the time he was doing his eating he kept on telling boring stories about his relatives!"

All Chester's vexation wanted to burst—but the only word that came out was "*Really!*"

"Loud-beak bum," Walter Water Snake muttered. "I know the type. Poor cricket. *Poor cricket!* What did you do?"

"I crawled out to the end of the branch and stayed there," said Chester. "And nobody even knew I was gone. Those birds carried on till the sun went down. And then they all fell asleep everywhere. I thought the whole tree would fall down! Even the sturdiest willow tree can only support so many birds."

"Where did you sleep, Chester?" Simon asked.

"Right out there—the little sleep I could get—in the crook of a twig, hanging on for dear life so I wouldn't fall into the brook. This morning I was up before anyone—I was so glad to see that sun! The birds started waking up, one by one, hiccupping and coughing, and making their tune-up morning chirps. I just left. I hopped down, branch by branch, and—left. Rude, I guess—just jumping out like that. I'll thank John Robin and Dorothy later. But—but—" Chester shook his head slowly. His antennae waved in wide, vague circles. "I knew this morning when I woke up

that the willow tree was not for me. It's not just the party. Sooner or later, the guests will leave. Don't guests always leave?"

"Not grackles," said Walter.

"Oh, he will, too. Eventually. But it's just that—well —I think that it would be very hard jumping, going up and down branches that aren't your own. And I think that they'd taste pretty bitter, the leaves of some-body else's tree."

In the midst of the sunny August morning another pool—a pool of gloomy silence—lay over Simon Turtle's pool.

"Poor cricket," said Walter. "Poor *cricket!*" And meant it. "*Ohhhhh—*" He lifted the saddest voice he had, and sang dejectedly:

A cricket moved to an old squirrel's nest—
To an old squirrel's nest moved he.
He thought he'd get some peace and rest—
But he just got company!

FIVE

Furry Folk

Chester's moping lasted—almost—till lunch. Simon Turtle, whenever he had to feel depressed, always tried to do it on a pleasant day, so he could get some sun at least. Walter Water Snake usually worked off his worry by doing figure eights on the water. He zigzagged there for about an hour—then Chester asked him please to stop. He was getting on the cricket's nerves, and also splashing him every time he closed a loop. As for Chester himself, in the past, if his mood turned bad —which wasn't too often—he'd jump his blues up onto the stump and sleep them off or wait for them to evaporate. But now—why, now there was no stump, no place to have a fit or a funk, alone, and then hop out into daylight again. Chester lay half in and half out of the crack at the top of Simon's log, with his head resting on his bell, and wondered if either he or it would ever ring with pleasure again.

"Yoo—"

"—hoo!"

Two "yoo-hoos," spoken almost together in piping soft voices, rose up to Chester. On the bank across the pool sat Henry Chipmunk and his sister, Emily. Even now, after all the time that they'd been friends, Chester still had trouble telling one from the other. They might have been twins, they were so much alike, although Emily was a little bit older than Henry. But Henry had a patch of light fur on the left side of his nose, and Emily's voice was a few notes higher. Chester had to look very close, or get them talking, to know for sure.

"Hi, Em. Hi, Hen," he said.

"I spent the night at Ellen's house—" That had to be Henry.

"—but this morning I certainly told him what happened!" squeaked the other excitedly.

When Tucker Mouse and Harry Cat had been up in Connecticut, rescuing the Old Meadow, the cat had been more or less adopted by Ellen, a girl who lived across Mountain Road. After Tucker and Harry had gone back to New York, Henry Chipmunk had been elected to do his duty as Ellen's pet. He sometimes slept over.

"We were down at your stump, Chester."

"Such a lot of birds there, Chester!"

"Dorothy Robin was talking to this big black chatterer—"

"A grackle," said Walter from the pool.

"Yes. Well, she was asking him if he didn't think that his friends downtown would be missing him—"

"They won't!" Walter sank down to his neck. "They may even be glad."

"Anyway, John and Dorothy didn't know where you were—"

"—so we guessed here—"

"—and here we are!"

"I see," said Chester. The chipmunks made him grin inside. They always did. It was sort of like being with someone small who was having such fun being busy and fussing that he'd just decided to double himself.

"And look what we've brought!" said the light-patch chipmunk excitedly.

"Since it's lunchtime—"

"—and also we thought that you might be depressed—"

"—since your home got wiped out—"

"—and the bush just bloomed this morning, too—"

"—after all the waiting we've done all summer!"

The two of them were bearing the burden of a big blackberry, holding it proudly, a gift from them both.

"Remember how much Mr. Mouse and Mr. Cat liked blackberries?" trilled High Voice.

"Well, over near our new home we've found the most *beautiful* bush!"

Em and Hen had formerly lived on the edge of the tumbledown cellar of the burned farmhouse, where long ago a human family had lived that owned the whole Meadow. But since that location had now become famous—and not altogether accurately—as the site of the old Hedley homestead, the chipmunks had

66

had to move. Too many sightseers. They'd followed the ruins of a fine stone wall, of which there are many in Connecticut, and discovered an even nicer home: a hole—in fact two holes which were joined—beneath a heavy, sheltering rock. And the entrance was well concealed and protected by a vigorous prickly old rosebush that had gone back to Nature ages past. Em and Hen, being rather timid souls, had grown very fond of that sturdy shrub, disheveled and wild as it might appear. They called it "Uncle" and felt, somehow, it went out of its way to keep them safe. To the left of Uncle—one stump and a white young poplar away—was the late-blooming blackberry bush.

Chester jumped, spread his wings, and coasted slowly above the pool, to land beside his friends. It felt good to fly; he decided there might be hope after all.

"Dig in!" said Light Patch.

"Yes, please! Yes, please!" the other dithered, in her giddy high voice.

While the three of them ate—and Simon and Walter had a taste as well—Chester told once more the story of the housewarming. That was how he had come to think of it: A Cricket's Tale of a Robin's Welcome, with lots of supporting characters. Chester Cricket had found that when something unpleasant happened to him, if he made a tale of it by telling it to some friends as a story—or best of all, if he sang it to himself as a song—then that sadness and unhappiness was easier on the heart. It sometimes even turned wonderful.

Walter and Simon, for instance, seemed to think the whole dismal experience was absolutely grand. They laughed and kept interrupting Chester to remind him of things—like the feathers which the birds had brought so he could build a nest—that the cricket had forgotten himself. Those poor, well-meant feathers! The second time around, they got to be even moldier.

The chipmunks relished the story, too. "My—" one would begin, and the other would end it, exclaiming, "—my!" Or "Good—" "—gracious!" "Oh—" "—dear!" By the time he arrived at his waking up that morning, Chester had learned to make little pauses so Emmy and Hen would be part of it all.

"Well, my goodness," said High Voice, "I never did hear such a thing—"

"—in our life! But what now?"

"Yes, what now? You aren't going back, are you?"

"No," said Chester. An antenna waved. He pecked at the blue ruins of the berry with his right front foot. "There must be some place in this Meadow for me to call home."

Both chipmunks burst out at once, *"Chester Cricket!"*

"Why don't you come—"

"—and live with us?"

"Wellll—" Chester's doubt drifted off, floating over the Meadow, in a single long note that sang I-don't-know.

But the chipmunks, mad with enthusiasm, bobbing like toys made of rubber and fur, wouldn't wait for one chirp of a cricket's uncertainty.

"We have *two* rooms, Chester—"

"—don't you see? And when I'm on duty, over at Ellen's—"

"—then you can have Henry's. And when he comes back—"

"There's plenty of room for all of us! And so nice—"

"We really have made it nice, Chester! There's a little bit of lawn—"

"—under Uncle, which we keep clipped—"

"—smooth! And dry ferns, to sleep on—"

"—we collect them ourselves—"

"—and then dry them especially—"

"—and keep them clean—"

"—oh, everything's clean—!"

"—immaculate!"

Chester's head was flicking left and right, to watch

them talk, like someone at a tennis match. "Hold up now!" he called. "You're going too fast."

"Please come, Chester—"

"—please!"

A silence—deciding—held everyone still.

"What do *you* think, Simon?" asked Chester. The old turtle shrugged his shell—which took quite a long time. "What about you, Walter?" said the cricket, who was still somewhat troubled. "What's your opinion?"

"I think it sounds divine!" said the snake. "A charming little country retreat."

The chipmunks looked at one another. "We don't live in retreats—"

"—we live right here."

"Okay. All right, my pint-sized eager beavers—"

"We're not beavers—"

"—we're chipmunks!"

"All right and okay!" Walter loomed up high and smiled down on Emmy and Hen. "I know who you are. You're tiny little furry folk, with hearts as big as all get-out. You take Creaky Cricket back with you and make him feel at home."

"I wish I knew when you were teasing," said Chester.

"Me? *Tease?*" If Walter had hands, he would have clapped one over his heart. "May all my skins fall off at once if ever this serpent should tease a friend!"

71

"Mmm," grumbled Chester skeptically. There was lots to doubt in the air today—although to anyone except a desperate homeless cricket who was talking to a zany water snake it might have seemed like any other ordinary morning.

"Scurry along now, Squeaky Creaker," Walt advised. "Em 'n' Hen are anxious to leave."

"I don't scurry!" declared Chester. "I hop, I jump— sometimes I fly—"

"These two will instruct you in scurrying." Walt laughed.

"We won't! He can go—"

"—any way that he wants!"

"And why do you call Chester Squeaker—"

"—and Creaker?"

"Because he's an insect," Walter explained. "He has the hard part of himself outside. An outside skeleton, one might say. And when he moves"—Walt lowered his head and spoke very confidentially—"he makes a little squeak. He goes '*Eek! eek! eek!*' Don't tell me you haven't noticed."

"We haven't. Do you—"

"—Chester, really? Go *eek?*"

"Of course!" Walter proclaimed. "He *eeks* all the time! Go on, Chester friend, bend a joint, stretch a leg—stretch lots of legs—and give us a little *eek,* why don't you?"

"I won't," said Chester, and hung his head. "I'm embarrassed."

"Har har. Har! har!" Walt zipped all around the pool in a circle. "Better hurry, too." He coasted and slowed, and stopped at the bank. "There's a shower coming."

"Yes, hurry—"

"—please, Chester!"

"We don't like—"

"—to get wet."

"I may as well," the cricket sighed. "I'm beginning to feel like a bump on that log. Bye, Simon. Bye, Walt. I'm off again."

"Off to your little green home in the West!" Walter Water Snake caroled poetically.

"We don't live in the West—"

"—we live halfway down the old stone wall!"

"And our home isn't green—"

"—it's the color of stone!"

"Beg pardon." Walter bowed. "But so long, anyway. So—" He stopped. "Come on, Simon—help me. So—"

"—long!" The turtle finished it for him, and laughed.

They watched as Chester hopped his hardest to keep

up with the chipmunks, who had a happy special bustle about them whenever they turned their noses toward home.

"Chester forgot his bell," said Simon.

"I don't think he really forgot it," said Walter.

"Poor soul." The turtle shook his glossy black head. "Do you think he ever will find a place?"

"And that reminds me, Turtle-urtle!" Walt knifed through the water, next to him. "There's something I want to discuss with you."

SIX

Home Life—and Too Much,
in Fact

And that afternoon, to the frisky delight of everyone who got caught in it, there *was* a brief shower—a downpour that lasted just long enough to rinse the day, what was left of it, and hang it out in the sunset to dry. Walter Water Snake and Simon Turtle barely noticed the rain. They were watery people and both of them enjoyed basking in either sunshine or shower. But not today. There was too much to talk about—plans to be laid—decisions taken. By twilight, they had made up their minds. Yet the stars found them still awake—too excited to sleep.

At sunup, after a fitful rest that lasted no more than a couple of hours, they both were awake and hard at work. Simon was busy, huffing and puffing, over and under and around his log, and Walt was dashing back and forth in the water, half out of sheer enthusiasm, but partly to clear debris away.

They both were so preoccupied that only by chance did Walt happen to look up and see on the bank— "Why, can this be? No, surely not. He went off yesterday to a cozy cottage, a lovely lair, a beautiful burrow. Oh no! But yes! It really is! It's—"

"Hi, Walter," said Chester, who was just too tired to be amused or angry or peeved, or anything else at Walter's way of speaking.

Walt raced like a cutter across the pool. "What are *you* doing here?"

The cricket shrugged—but only one shoulder, things seemed so hopeless. "I don't have any place else to go." He glanced around—at the log, the pool. "What are you two doing? What's all this stuff?"

"Why—why"—Walter Water Snake seemed at a loss for words, which was very unlike him—"we're making boats!"

"Boats?"

"Aren't we, Simon?" Walter demanded. "Making boats—"

"Oh, boats! To be sure!" the turtle agreed. "Comes over us every August, it does—this urge to build boats."

76

Home Life—and Too Much, in Fact

"Look at this." Walter nosed a piece of bark toward the bank. The pool's surface was littered with chips of wood and bark. "This elegant sliver of bark is a boat." He gentled it around and around, then out the channel that led to the brook, where the current took it. "And there she goes! Away down our own bucolic stream—but soon to be joined, after travels through numerous little towns, to the ever-flowing, majestic Connecticut River—and then—O grandeur!—with a whoosh and a rush and sploosh, the glory of Long Island Sound! Just think of it, Cricket! The poetry of it—the beauty! It makes the heart swell."

"It makes the head ache, the way you describe it," said Chester.

But Walter, whose mind was flying high, would not be stopped. "And along with toy boats when the fit is upon us, we make—we make"—he glanced around, discovered a chunk of floating wood, which didn't look all that big to Chester, and slithered up on top of it—"we make *boat* boats!" And promptly capsized, which wasn't a serious accident, for a water snake.

"Very impressive," said Chester, when Walter came up, spluttering joyfully.

"Just watch! Just watch!" The snake tried again, and this time he managed to stay afloat. By using the

end of his tail like an oar, he even was able to paddle himself in leisurely circles around the pool. "Just look! Am I grace? I am athletic grace! I am poetry in motion!"

"You're crazy," said Simon.

"Now you, Crunchy Cricket!" Walter beached his homemade canoe below Chester. "Jump on!"

"Oh, Walt," Chester groaned. "I don't feel like a boat ride."

"See these fangs?" The water snake reared up, made his head level with Chester, and showed the cricket two really astonishing, long, curved teeth.

"Very scary," said Chester.

"You hop on my pleasure craft before I sink 'em into you!"

"Oh, all right." Chester did as he was told. And found that the boat was much more suitable for a cricket than for an overactive water snake. "You wouldn't really bite me, Walter, would you?"

"No, never. Never!" Walt shook his head. "But I have to pull rank sometimes to remind myself that I'm terrifying. At least that's what some dopey humans think. There"—he sank to his nose and rocked Chester gently on the rhythmical billows that flowed back and forth across Simon's Pool—"isn't that comfy, now?"

Chester stretched himself out. In fact, it felt so delectable, he stretched each leg out separately. "Quite nice," he admitted. "Delightful, I must say. Very restful."

"You look as if you need a rest." Walt peered at Chester, examining him—very doctorish. His beady eyes, if only they behaved themselves, were highly scientific.

"I didn't sleep a wink," yawned Chester.

"More birds?"

"No birds."

"Then elephants? Zebras? Kangaroos?" Walter searched for unusual animals, and found the strangest ones of all. "*Chipmunks*, perhaps?"

"I didn't dare fall asleep," confessed Chester. "Emmy and Hen said I snored."

"Poor *cricket!*" Walter exclaimed. He found a position that suited him and just settled back to relax. Walter could do that with water—just turn it into furniture that fitted him any way he wished. "Let's hear it all. Just start from Stump One."

"Stump One is squashed," said Chester. "I'll start from when we left yesterday. Well—" The deep breath he drew now—the breath to tell all—was a little bit sadder than the one he had drawn just the day before.

"We scurried on home, with the two of them urging me please to keep up—it was going to rain. So then we got there. And oh, Walter—oh, Simon—you just ought to see their lawn!"

"But what about Uncle?" Simon asked.

"Oh, Uncle—I forgot," said the cricket. "He's a grand old rosebush—he really is. Very casual, very easygoing. Just lets himself climb and spread as he wants, every which way. Very informal he is. And believe you me!—Uncle Rosebush is absolutely the last informal soul that I saw yesterday! 'Cause behind good old Uncle—"

"I see it coming!" caroled Walter. "Behind good old Uncle, the chip and the munk have their lawn."

"Do they *ever!*" said Chester. "And are they ever proud of it! I have to admit, though, it's beautiful— that is, if you like grass so well tended it has to be treated like fragile green glass. You know that golf course, Walter? South of the Meadow?"

"I know it," said Walter. "But I don't golf much. Play a lot of tennis, but—"

"*Anyway*—the chipmunks' lawn would make the neatest green on that golf course look like a patch of untended prairie. They bite it once a week."

"The chipmunks bite their lawn?" This bit of information astonished even Walt Water Snake. He keeled over backwards and disappeared. And stayed under for quite a long time.

"Walter?" Chester tapped the water. "Walt Water Snake?"

"You called?" The snake popped up again and rested his head on the chunk of wood—now Chester's boat— where the cricket was floating. "Do you mean to tell me, Cracklin' Cricket, that Emmy and Hen chew on their lawn?"

"It's the only way they can keep it trimmed just so. And 'just so,' they told me, is how they like it. Not too long, not too short—"

—"just so." Walter saw it all. "Oh boy! oh boy! Oh me! oh my!"

"I was invited to join them next Thursday, biting the lawn. That's when they do it: every Thursday at ten o'clock. The weather permitting, I suppose."

"The sweetness of it! The tenderness!" Walter saw even more. "Just think—like two little brown sheepies, munching away. Next Christmas, somebody should give them a doll's-house lawnmower."

"I wanted to see this fabulous turf up close," said Chester, "but as I was bending down, they both squeaked at me, 'Please don't—' '—step on the grass!'

And honestly, Walter, my feet aren't really all that big. I wouldn't have left a dent in their lawn. But to hear the way they were hollering, anybody'd suspect that I was a June bug wearing wooden shoes. I hopped quick back on the path, I can tell you."

"They have a path?" Walter asked.

"A beautiful path! Made out of twenty-six perfect white stones, curving up to their front door. I know there are twenty-six, too, because they told me so— twice. It took them six months to find just the right stones, in the brook. They have to match exactly, you see."

"Imagine! Twenty-six perfect white stones," echoed Walter. "It sounds just like a fairy tale! I'm surprised they didn't use bread crumbs."

"The birds would have eaten the bread crumbs," said Chester. "And besides"—he cleared his throat— "you can't polish bread crumbs."

"They *don't!*" Walter exclaimed.

"Every Wednesday. Weather permitting. At three in the afternoon. They said so. With nice dry little ferns that they save especially for polishing."

"Could you get me an invitation?"

"To polish the path? You *want* one—?"

84

"Har har." Walt rocked Chester's boat so vigorously that the cricket almost fell off.

"Oh, Walter—you get me so mad sometimes," said Chester—and almost meant it, too—as he tried to keep from falling in.

Like many snakes, Walter Water Snake could do with his wiggling what most animals—and a few human beings, the gifted ones—can do with their hands: he could express the most subtle and wide-ranging emotions. The hypnotic swaying, just now, of his whole upper half above the water suggested admiration and awe—and perhaps a little twitch of doubt. "If the yard and the path were so perfect"—he sighed and looked toward heaven—"the mind boggles to think what the house must be like!"

"It's beautiful!"

Walter loomed over Chester eagerly. "Tell me! Tell me! Tell me!"

"Everything"—the cricket paused—"is in place."

The looming became more impatient. "Well? *Well?*"

"Well, that's it. Everything is just so. I felt—that is, even before they told me not to—that I really shouldn't touch anything."

"They told you to keep your feet off their house?"

85

"Not in so many words," Chester tried to explain. "But I guess I'm just a touchy person. You know, Walter, these front feet of mine"—he wiggled two feet to demonstrate—"they're almost as agile as hands. And I do like to handle things, too."

"I don't have hands *or* feet!" said Walter. "And I get by."

"Well, of course," agreed Chester. "But if you do have a hand or a foot—"

"—or a fang—"

"—or a fang—you might as well use it, is my philosophy. Well, not the fang, exactly."

"On special occasions, I use my fangs!" boasted Walter. "Like building boats." He winked at Simon. (Or would have, if he'd had an eyelid.)

"Anyway, I like to touch things!" Chester said. "I like to pick things up and hold them close and look at them. You get the feel of the world that way. But when I picked up the rose blossom—"

"*What* blossom?"

"It's one of Uncle's most beautiful blossoms. They saved it from last spring. In the middle of the living room—they call it the living room, although Henry sleeps there, the room just inside the door—in there they've got this big table. It's made of a section of branch, gnawed smooth on each side. And, Walter, I mean *smooth!* What those chipmunks can do with their teeth is amazing."

"Little dental homemakers, they are," Walt observed.

"Yes, and right smack in the center—the centerpiece —of this very carefully gnawed maple table is Uncle's loveliest, biggest blossom. In a tasteful arrangement of four green leaves."

"Oh!" exclaimed Walter. "I'm going to faint!" And he fainted. At least he collapsed beneath the surface. And blew a few bubbles. And reappeared. "They're into flowers. I knew it!"

"They certainly are!" Chester Cricket went on. "Their two rooms are simply papered with petals! There's some of Uncle's best petals, of course, but there's also purple ones, from irises, and yellow daisy and crocus petals. The red ones from Uncle are the best, but they've got dried petals tacked up on their walls from every single kind of flower that grows in this whole Meadow! They start collecting and drying in March—they told me so."

Simon Turtle sighed and shook his head—at the wonder and the diligence of little animals. He'd been listening silently all this while. "But how do they tack them up?"

"With Uncle's thorns. But they never pick one—

they swore to that. He just seems to know. Whenever they need a thorn or two, to pin up a new petal, they find some out on the lawn in the morning. He's wonderful! He gives them whole blossoms, he gives them petals, he gives them leaves—and then thorns to hold it all together. I think he must love them an awful lot. Of course, being a plant, he never says much."

"Itsy-bitsy chipsy munks! I love them, too," said Walter. "More. More! Tell us *more*—of the tasteful decor that the chipmunks adore! How's the ceiling? The floor? Are there knickknacks galore? Wow! *Sssst!* I really feel great today!" Walt felt so great that he streaked up out of the water, turned a somersault in the air, and—straight as an arrow—plunged back in. He came up where Chester hadn't expected, behind the boat. "Some dive, huh? I'll show you a triple next time. But what else about Emmy and Hen—what else?"

"They have a fireplace—"

"That's good to hear! A fireplace is cozy at least."

"It's never lit."

"Oh, gosh!" Walter Water Snake sank down in despair. "An unlit hearth. That's sad, sad, *sad!*"

"They say it would smoke up the flowers, and maybe leave soot on the stones. They live in this old stone wall, you know, and on the inside those stones are *clean!*"

"I'll bet."

"But the fireplace is very pretty. There's little dry branches crisscrossed in it, and crumpled dry leaves underneath, with a fan of ferns in the back. All it needs is a match."

"I'm going to slither over there—"

"Oh no, you're not!" said Simon Turtle.

"I'll swipe a lighted cigarette—from a picnicker, whom I'll terrify first, of course—"

"You'll stay right in that pool where you belong. You'd scare the poor dears to death. So you didn't feel too much at home there, Chester?"

"I didn't dare to turn around! For fear of knocking down pussy willows. Whenever there's room between the blossoms, there are pussy-willow wands. I sat in a corner for an hour or so, and then it began to rain."

"Don't tell me their house leaks."

"Gracious no! The rain wouldn't dare leak on Emmy and Hen. But I like these sudden summer showers. It always feels as if someone decided to take a bath—all at once. I like to go for a hop in the rain. Especially toward the end of one, when the sun comes out and everything begins to glisten. I love to jump in the sparkle of things. And yesterday we had a rainbow. Only a short one, but long enough to make my wish."

"I thought everybody packed his bags and went off to look for the pot of gold," said Simon Turtle.

"Oh, I don't believe that. There's no pot of gold at the end of the rainbow. But I do believe you can wish on one."

"I'll bet I know what your wish was, Chancy Chester!"

"Don't tell if you do!" the cricket warned. "It won't work if you say it. So, anyway, I had my hop and came back to Littleville."

"Is *that* what they call it?" There seemed to be nothing of Walter underwater; the whole of him was stretched up in the air.

"No, *I* do," said Chester. "But don't you dare tell them! I wouldn't hurt their furry feelings for the tastiest leaves in Connecticut. They were always extremely polite and nice. Even when insisting I wipe my feet."

"Let me guess," said Walter. "You came back from your walk in the rain—"

"—and my feet were dirty. Right. That is, there were two or three specks of mud, which I barely could see— on two or three feet—but Emily could. Oh, could she ever! As soon as I hopped in the door—"

"With a cheery 'Hi, Itsy! Hi, Bitsy!' no doubt."

Home Life—and Too Much, in Fact

"I didn't say *that!*" declared Chester. "I didn't have time to say a word before Emily started to wring her hands. She's very good at that, Emily is. Henry prefers to shake his head and say 'Tsk! tsk!' Well, one said, 'Oh dear, you've tracked—' and the other one finished it '—in dirt!'"

"O horror! O terror! O vilest of crimes!"

"Oh, Walt, keep quiet!" Chester Cricket exploded. "Do you want to hear the story or not?"

"I do," said Walter gravely. "I'm deeply moved. And I bow most low in apology." He bowed most low—so low, indeed, that he disappeared from sight. For a while. "Okay, I'm back. So *then* what happened?" He rested his chin on the bow of the boat.

"I was informed, very courteously, that there was a mat outside. Not outside the door, mind you. Oh no! It was just before you reached the lawn. They like for people to wipe their feet before they step on the polished stone path."

"*Ohhhh—*" Walter began.

"Are you going to sing something?"

"Maybe later. If the spirit moves." The water snake coyly twitched his tail, sucked on a fang, and winked at Chester. "Please go on."

"I cleaned my feet on the mat they'd made—knotted out of dry fern, and very nice—and scraped off the mud

91

on a root of Uncle's that stuck above ground. Which I'm sure he didn't mind me doing. As a matter of fact, from the rustling going on all around, my guess is he found me hilarious. I didn't, though. I found me *absurd!* Standing there and balancing as I tried to wipe off all my feet on a fern!"

"I don't find you absurd." As quick as a flash—but not to bite—Walter struck and gave Chester a peck of a kiss on the head. "I find you delightful. Pray continue."

"Dinner time, it was by then. We washed our paws —that is, they did. *I* washed my two front feet again— in the chipmunk's thimble. And don't look at me with your snake eyes, Walter! They *do* have a thimble, which they keep all polished up with ferns. You know that old lady—the one who always wears the red shawl, on the hottest days, too; she comes once a week, and sits on a bench in Pasture Land, and sews all afternoon —you know her? Well, last July she lost a thimble, and she's never going to find it again—"

"—because Emry and Henly now have a silver cistern in their house!"

"Exactly! Which they fill with fresh water whenever it rains."

"I see it! Oh, I do see it!" said Walter. His gaze was

at something awesome. "The beauty of littleness! Little chipmunks! Little thimbles! Little wishes! And real *big* happiness! Oh, I love it! More! *More!*"

"We washed. And then wiped our paws, feet, whatever, on clean fern towels they have stacked by the thimble-cistern-sink."

"Fern towels, fern towels." Walter seemed dazed by the thought. "I never knew fern was so useful."

"That isn't all. We sat at the table and ate off doilies made—"

"—of fern!"

"—and wiped our mouths with napkins—"

"—of fern! Hallelujah! And hooray for fern! That's what we'll call the chips' hideaway—Fern Lawn! How's that?"

"Terrific, Walter!" Chester almost forgot how tired he was in the rush of Walter's enthusiasm. "They may not be so mad at me for sneaking out this morning when they find we've invented a name for their place."

"You snuck out?"

"Yes, while they were still asleep. Of course, I—who was so dead-tired my antennae were dragging, after my night in the willow tree—I didn't sleep at all."

"Why not?" Walter wondered. "There were no fern mattresses? No fern blankets? Fern pillows? Green little fern dreams to dance in your head?"

"I snore!" declared Chester.

"A cricket snores?" Walter looked at Simon. "It must sound like a fluttering leaf in the breeze."

"Like a buzz saw, I sound! Like a Mack truck! Like a hurricane roaring through a redwood forest! Like the subway—!"

"They said *that?*"

"No. They tapped me gently on my third left leg and said, 'Chester dear, would you please—' '—roll over?' 'Neither one of us—' '—can sleep a wink.' And the thing is—this really is what did me in—*they snore!*"

"O bitter irony!" Walter lifted his eyes toward the sky—where there was no bitter irony, so he smiled down on Chester again. "And what do *they* sound like, might I ask?"

Chester giggled. "I have to admit, it's very nice—like two cute music boxes."

"I love it!" Walter thrashed his tail with delight. "Two musical little chipmunk snores—in a little house by itself at night—with the little darkness tight all around. I do love it!"

"And they sound absolutely identical, too! Exactly the same! I couldn't find a speck of difference."

"So this is how you spent the night? In a scientific

investigation, pacing from one room into the other in a vain attempt to find a single speck of difference between the beautiful, musical snores of Emily and Henry Chipmunk?"

"You might put it like that," said Chester. "I don't know anyone but you who would—except maybe a mischievous bat—but, yes, that's how I spent the night. Anyway, though, I never could live with them. I just felt—with everything being so perfect, with the ferns and the flowers and the stones just so—I felt—"

"Maladjusted!" The water snake did a flip-flop. "It's something I rarely suffer from. But I know all about maladjustment, I do! That little boy, Jaspar—the one who helped you to save the Old Meadow—one day I heard him lamenting the trials of family life with his best friend, Ben Thompson. And he was complaining about just the same things that are bugging you. In Jaspar's case, it was his own devoted mama, not persnickety chipmunks, who was causing him such distress. She made him wipe feet, she made him wash hands. 'She's making me maladjusted!' he screamed. Poor soul. You should have seen him chewing his gum and tearing his hair. I hope she let him snore, at least."

"Mamas usually do," said Simon Turtle, from ancient wisdom.

"I learned a lot about maladjustment that day,"

Home Life—and Too Much, in Fact

Walter went on. "As a matter of fact—as a matter of fact!—*ohhhh—!*"

Chester put some grumpiness into his voice. "Now it comes:

> "*A cricket lived in a neat chip's lair—*
> *In a sweet munk's lair lived he.*
> *But he was maladjusted there—*
> *And snored most dreadfully!*"

SEVEN

Donald Dragonfly

"Well, I have to admit"—Chester Cricket lay back and just drifted—"it's an awfully nice day to be homeless on."

For several hours, the three Meadow dwellers had gone boating. At least Walt and Chester went boating. Simon Turtle, with that solid black shell of his, was too heavy to float on the pieces of wood that were circling slowly around his pool. When he made the offhanded suggestion—"Might just lumber up and bite me off a big chunk near the top of my log"—Walter Water Snake glared at him sternly, behind Chester's back. Simon mumbled, "Oh," and contented himself with offering bits of nautical advice, whenever the other two would listen.

The cricket invented a game he liked. He spread out his wings and turned himself into a sturdy little workable sail in the breeze. Walter Water Snake thought

that was wonderful. He shouted, "Hey! Great!"—
found a hunk of wood, slithered up on it, and hoisted
his tail straight up in the air. It made the skinniest,
silliest sail—like an upright rope—that was ever seen
in Connecticut. And keeping his whole lower half like
that, so rigid and stiff, in such a difficult position, was
hard work for even the most supple creature. Walter
toppled over constantly, with a whoop and laugh as he
splashed out of sight. He made up his mind that instead of playing "sail," he'd play "shipwreck," and
enjoyed his own game very much.

Chester called his skiff the *West Wind*—since that
happened to be blowing—and Walter called his the
Curlicue, named after himself, of course.

But evening came, and along with the shadows, in
a twilight that lacked all coziness, the cricket's gloom
returned. He eyed the log. "I guess I'll have to spend
the night in that narrow old crack again."

"No!" blurted Walt. "We need some more time. I
mean—I mean—it's uncomfortable. Isn't it, Chester?
Uncomfortable?"

"Well, yes," began Chester, "but if that's all there
is—"

"That isn't all there is!" said Walter. "There's—
there's—the *West Wind!* A sleeper ship, if ever I saw
one. She may not have staterooms or bunk beds, Ches-

ter—or even a hammock, spun by a spider—but she'll rock you asleep on the bosom of the deep, ol' pal. Won't she, Simon? Your pool *is* the deep."

"It's deep enough for me, ol' pal." Simon treated himself to a long and leisurely yawn. "And time to be turning in." He crept to his favorite resting place. The old turtle had several comfortable beds, but this time of year there was one special spot, where the bank overhung his pool and the mud was soft and oozy and good, that felt most right, most covered and snug. He stretched his legs, then pulled them in, beneath his shell. His head was last. A final "Good night" echoed out in the dark.

For the first time ever, Chester envied his friend his safe, secure shell. When all else failed, that at least was a very private home.

Walter Water Snake whisked to a clump of reeds where he usually spent the night. "You get some rest now, Chester. And don't *worry!* Things are bound to work out. Just trust me."

"I do," said Chester. And added under his breath, "I guess." He wondered just how many crickets had ever put their faith in a snake—and one with a devilish sense of humor at that.

He was tired enough, poor cheerless Chester—more exhausted that night than he'd ever been. Yet he still couldn't sleep. It wasn't his boat. As Walter had said, the rocking and bobbing was very restful. It lulled him sweetly, and the stars seemed to sway, as the *West Wind* drifted. Perhaps it was just those August stars that were keeping him awake. They seemed so huge this time of year, like lamps that someone had hung in the air. And, as always in August—*there!* one went—the sky was full of shooting stars. In New York, on his expedition to the Museum of Natural History, Chester Cricket had been taken to the Planetarium, which was right next door. And there he had heard that every August the earth passed through a shower of meteors, and they were the shooting stars. He sort of believed that. But also there was a legend among all insects that shooting stars were fireflies that had flown too high, and he sort of believed that, too. Whatever they were, falling stars could keep a soul awake—sometimes in the pure joy of watching and waiting for one, sometimes in the sadness that beauty can give when a man, or a cricket, has trouble.

Against his will, Chester leaped from the boat to the bank. He knew where he was going, all right, and knew that he really didn't want to go there—but didn't know how to stop himself.

One summer there'd been a bad fire over on Mountain Road. Nobody was hurt, but a whole house burned down. And the afternoon after the accident, the family that lived there—every single member of it—had gathered in front of the smoking ruins. Chester Cricket remembered that sad scene well. There were two children, a boy and a girl, and the man and his wife. No one said a word. They all just stood there, silently staring at smoking embers.

In just such a mood of helpless, hopeless emptiness Chester Cricket was drawn through the radiant, soft summer night to his stump. He felt like a little mechanical insect with no choice at all, as he leaped and landed, leaped and landed, beside the brook on the old familiar path. John Robin had told him the stump was in ruins. He'd seen it himself; the whole Meadow knew it. Still, he had to go back again.

Late moonlight silvered the tumbled wood. Because of the way the trees grew close, or the turn it made, or the rush of the current, the brook made a faint ghost-echo here. The water was talking to Chester's stump—still talking, the way it always had, but now in a lower, more private tone.

"Why," said the cricket aloud, astonished, "it's beautiful!"

He jumped to one side and took another careful look. Dark fragments where the top was crushed stood up like towers, like battlements, against the star-struck

sky. The stump was transformed. And it seemed to Chester as if the change had taken place not because of some silly accident but as if the magician's hand of Nature had passed above his well-known house and conjured it into something else. His home it would never be again—Chester stared at the stump as if in its ruin it somehow was new—and never belong to him anymore. "But, still," he murmured to himself, "it always can be beautiful."

He spoke one word aloud, "Brookview," then began the hop back to Simon's Pool.

And halfway there, a flicker of misty light, like a tiny mooncloud hovering above the brook, caught his eye. Entranced by the sight, the cricket paused. The Meadow had many such gifts to give, unexpected jolts of sudden wonder, and Chester instinctively pressed each one as deep as he could in his memory.

He was trying to decide if the mooncloud was drifting on the brook's surface—or was it a patch of mist trapped in a spider's web?—when a dry squeak of voice asked, "Chister?"

"Donald," said Chester, "is that you?"

"It's me, Chister. Jump out. Be kirful! My twig's pritty little."

Chester saw a thin branch, like a finger of darkness pointing out in the soft darkness of night. Donald's voice and the cloud of light came from its end. The cricket jumped and landed beside Donald Dragonfly. They were only an inch above the brook, which swayed beneath them, until the branch had steadied itself.

"Why, it's only the moon on your wings," said Chester. "I thought that light was mist, or something."

"I kin make myself look like mist," said Donald, "I kin fade in real good, whin I want to, Chister. It's how I stay alive."

"And this is where you live, Donald?"

"*Yiss!* Right here in this fork of my twig. Not minny folks know it." Donald gave off the puff of a dragonfly's laughter. "You like it?"

"It's marvelous!" said Chester Cricket, holding on tight to the jiggling twig. "Very safe here, I imagine."

"*Kik! kik! kik!*" That was how Donald laughed. "It's safe, all right! Thir's not minny can balance here." Very hard to describe, a dragonfly's laughter, but very infectious: the cricket found himself chuckling, too.

"I barely can, myself."

"I heered about all your troubles, Chister. The whole Middow's talkin'. The way you can't find a new home."

Donald Dragonfly

"I'll just bet," said the cricket.

"And I want you to know"—Donald took in a breath, to help the timid truth along—"you kin live with me here, Chister Cricket! Jist is long is you want. Feriver, even!"

"Why, Donald Dragonfly!" Chester gasped. The dragonfly had a reputation, among the reeds, along the grass, for being—"eccentric," a few people said, and "peculiar," said others. But everyone, insects, animals —even the fish in the brook who knew him—agreed that he was solitary. To be asked to share a home with Donald: "I honestly don't know what to say."

"It's Augist now, Chister, and a bug's most a bug in Augist. Jist listen to ivrybody! *Kik! kik! kik!* The world's ours ivry year this time."

In the dark that trembled with pale moonlight, Chester Cricket was learning a lot. "I didn't know that you thought about things like this, Donald. August —and the time of year."

"Will, what ilse should a bug think about, Chister? Till me."

The cricket shrugged. "Nothing, I guess. I've been thinking about stuff like that the whole night myself."

"Innyway, it's not a good time to be by yersilf," said Donald. "Yer wings kin drop off."

Donald Dragonfly

Chester shook his head. "You're quite a soul, I have to admit. You're not—" He stopped. As always—or at least, as often—good manners seemed to come too late.

"Oh, you kin say it," the dragonfly squeaked. "I know what people think of me. They think I'm titched. And you know something, Chister? They're right. *Kik! kik! kik!* It's the light is does it. I bin titched so often —my wings, I mean—and by so many diffrint kinds of light—by sunlight, and moonlight, and starlight, too —why, 'course I'm titched!"

"I think your wings are beautiful, Donald! And the colors that dance all over them—they're the very most beautiful things in the Meadow."

'Will, I think so, too," agreed Donald. "Ixcipt you have to pay a price. And the price is that I'm titched, I guiss. And as far as being beautiful goes, I think the music that you kin make goes ivry bit is far is my light!"

"Oh no—" began Chester.

"We could find out!" the dragonfly interrupted him. He was shivering with excitement—so much that his wings shed a cascade of silver drops. "If you were to come and live with me—will, I could flicker my wings in the light and make my colors look like your music. Wowy me! *Kik! kik! kik!* How would that be, Chister?"

"Terrific, Donald," said Chester. "But . . ." What-

ever the "but" was, it made him pause. "I just think
—somehow—you make colors, and I make music,
and—"

"Yiss, I see." Donald nodded philosophically. "It's
bitter to keep thim apart."

"Most times," said the cricket. "But *some* times,
of course, we could do it together."

"Fer spicial occasions!"

"*Yiss!* I mean, yes."

"You still could live with me, Chister, though."

"I could," agreed Chester, "but—" And this "but"
—the biggest—needed no explanations.

"I know," said Donald. "I'm a loner, too. But I jist
had to *ask*."

"I will always be grateful," said Chester Cricket.
He hesitated, but then decided to speak his whole
heart. "And, Donald, after this talk we've had—which
I really enjoyed very much, more even than I can say
—I always will think of you as being my secret best
friend."

They touched wings, which is something that insects do.

EIGHT

The Lady Beatrice

The next morning, back at Simon's Pool, the cricket didn't tell either the snake or the turtle about what had happened the night before. It was too private—just insect to insect, one might say.

However, the problem still remained. In fact, it stayed around all day.

Walt Water Snake didn't seem too upset—impatient, if anything, Chester thought. He was frisking and fidgeting all afternoon, as if he simply couldn't wait for Chester to leave on another trial flight toward home.

"Surely *some* kindly soul will offer you a night's lodging," said Walter. "As a matter of fact, I do believe that I spy a kindly soul—who looks like a whole week's worth of lodging—waddling toward me this very minute!"

Chester glanced at the bank. "Shh!" he whispered.

"She'll hear you. You know how sensitive Beatrice is."

"Why, Madame Plumage"—Walter made a very elaborate bow, which had at least three curves in it—"I just this second was saying to Chester, I wish those elegant fowl the Pheasants would come toddling over and pay us a visit."

Ambling along, by the side of the brook, were Beatrice Pheasant and her husband, Jerome. Now, it is well known that in most pheasant families the male bird always grows the most beautiful plumage. It's his right—Nature says so. And, indeed, in the case of Jerome and Beatrice, if you looked very closely, you would see that the gold and the amber and the brown—and perhaps a hidden trace of green—that his feathers contained were more brilliant than hers. Yet, somehow, Beatrice seemed the more grand. Perhaps it was just that she always walked first, and talked first, and spoke with such quiet authority. Or maybe her size, which was very impressive, made her look rather special. Whatever the reason, and despite what Nature might say, Beatrice was the Pheasant who favored the Old Meadow with her presence, and Jerome was a pheasant, her husband, whom everyone tended to like and forget. (On most matters, in fact, Beatrice Pheasant liked to have the last word, and not leave it to Nature or anyone else whose views might differ from her own.)

The Lady Beatrice

She cleared her throat and spoke with a slight but
becoming warble. "Jerome and I were out for our constitutional—" By which she meant a high-class walk
that the Pheasants took late every afternoon. "And we
thought we'd just drop round and see how dear Chester
was faring. Didn't we, Jerome?"

"Mhmm."

"He's faring lousy!" said Walter, from the pool. For
some reason known only to himself—or perhaps to
another water snake—Walter's speech had a curious
tendency to become somewhat crude whenever he
talked to Beatrice. "Tell 'em, Cricket. Unburden your
woes on these sympathetic listeners."

"*You* tell 'em," said Chester. "You're enjoying my
woes a lot more than I am."

So Walter did just that: with many a flourish and
many a flip—a few of which splashed water all over
the Pheasants, but only by accident—he narrated Chester's night in the willow and his night in the wall.

Beatrice found it all very distressing. She murmured
"Shocking! How very common!" when she heard about
all those party-flocking birds, and muttered something
to the effect that she herself had been told by the chipmunks to stay off the grass—and none too politely, at
that. Jerome seemed a little more amused. He had a
kind of private laugh, a cackle or chuckle, that showed

how much he enjoyed the adventures, but Beatrice, with a polite look, managed to silence him before he could start to laugh out loud.

When Walter finished speaking, she tsked and tutted —which she did very well—and scratched the earth firmly with her sharp right claw. "Most upsetting, I'm sure. But the answer's perfectly obvious." With a swish of her tail—which she swished very often—she solved all problems. "Chester dear, you must live with us!"

"Oh—uh—I—" Chester looked one way, then another, and his six legs started to creep backwards. "I'd hate to be a nuisance, Beatrice."

"Nonsense, Chester! No nuisance at all. We've oodles of room. Don't we, Jerome?"

"Mhmm."

"There are five tuffets now, in the Towers, I believe. Are there five, Jerome? Or six?"

"Hmm?" '

"Tuffets, dear! In the Towers? Five or six?"

"I lost count," said Jerome.

"What's the Towers?" Walter asked.

"That's what we call our place," explained Beatrice. "Tuffet Towers. There's the tuffet that faces south— we call that Sunnyreach—and the one to the north— Chillington—and two that we just call the east and west wings. And the big one in the middle, of course

—*the* Tower—which gives the whole thing its name. That's five." She sighed, somewhat weary. "But there may be one or two others elsewhere. It makes one long for the simple old days."

"And how, might I ask, are all these tuffets connected?" asked Walt.

"With thatch, Mr. Water Snake—all with thatch. A little thatch here, a little thatch there—"

"Here a thatch, there a thatch, everywhere a thatch-thatch—"

"Walter!" Chester whispered. "Be quiet, please."

But Beatrice Pheasant hadn't noticed, or else she pretended not to notice. With a well-bred pheasant you never know. "So space is no problem. Do come!" she urged.

Chester had his doubts about Tuffet Towers. It wasn't in Tuffet Country, he knew. That part of the Meadow was near his stump. There was space and grass between most of the tuffets, and although they hadn't been planted in rows, there seemed to be some kind of order there, as if Nature herself had made a garden, with a subtle design that only she knew. But the Pheasants lived off to the north and the west, past Emmy and Hen's stone wall, in a woodsy and wild location. It never had really been cultivated as garden or orchard for the old homestead, and even the long-gone cows never browsed there. It was simply an area of the Old Meadow that had grown up alone, and been let go.

"You'll love it!" said Beatrice to Chester. "So rustic and free, we feel. It's all very unspoiled."

"Many mountain lions up there?" said Walter Water Snake.

"Mr. Water Snake—really!"

"Wolves? Bears?"

"You're joking, of course." The pheasant managed a ripple of giggle.

"Walter *never* jokes!" said Chester.

Beatrice, who was used to getting her way, scratched the ground again. She had a slow but determined scratch, as if her way was somewhere in the earth down there, and sooner or later she meant to get it. "And Miss Jenny'll take care of you."

Walter, Simon, and Chester all looked at each other—and then at the Pheasants. "Who's that?"

"She's our field mouse," explained Beatrice. "We've had her for years. Have we not, Jerome?"

"Mhmm."

Simon Turtle gasped. "You don't mean little Genevieve Field Mouse? From years ago? I remember her! What a darling she was! So rambunctious and funny. Good grass, I'd almost forgotten her. How is she now?"

"She's *old*," said Jerome.

"I should think so, indeed." Simon smiled as his eyes looked at nothing and saw the past. "My stars— we were young together."

"And turtles are older than anyone," observed Walter Water Snake.

"Such pretty silvery fur she had." Simon felt the sweet hurt of things gone by.

"It's all gray now!" said Jerome.

"Just how far along *is* Miss Mouse?" Walter inquired.

"Why, Jenny"—Simon reckoned the time. "Of course, even then I had a few years on her—I've got a few years on most Meadow folk—but Jenny—twenty, twenty-five, thirty—"

"Mmm!" Walter murmured appreciatively. "That's a ripe old age for a field mouse."

Beatrice, too, was becoming nostalgic. "She came to us the same day we moved under our very first tuffet."

"And she wasn't young then." Jerome did a little scratching himself. "And that's *ages* ago!"

"Not 'ages,' dear," his wife corrected.

"Just what," Walter went on, "does Miss Jenny Field Mouse do for you?"

"She gets lost a lot."

"Oh, Jerome! Don't exaggerate! *Really*, my dear!

The Lady Beatrice

A slight tendency to wander away," Beatrice explained. "That's all it is. She fetches, carries—makes the beds."

"When she can remember where they are!"

"I'd be lost without her."

"We get lost trying to find her sometimes," said Jerome.

"I've heard quite enough," the pheasant decided. "Now come along, Chester. We'll show you the Towers while there's still enough light. It'll just be splendid, having you there. And also, my dear, there's one wee chore you can do for us. I'll tell you about it on the way home. Jerome—follow me!" With great dignity—she'd been practicing all her life—Beatrice swiveled and swung around, her plumage ruffed and head thrown back, Jerome in tow, and began a stately plod toward home.

Chester Cricket felt helpless. As happens so often, he had let himself be defeated again by the kindness of friends. "Okay—let's go." He shrugged his first shoulders, sighed at Simon, made a face at Walter, and, hopping his hardest, brought up the rear of the pheasant parade.

"Shh!" Walter hissed at the turtle, to warn him. "Be quiet, now. We can't start work till they're out of sight." By craning up, he could just see over the edge of the bank. "I daresay before another day has passed we shall hear the tale of Chester Crickety and Field Mouse Rickety." He shook his head and laughed at the three receding figures. "Chester's jumping looks grim. There's no joy in that jump. The poor *cricket!* And there he goes."

NINE

Tuffet Towers

And—"Here he comes!" Walt said the next morning.

His head was still craned to see over the bank. A stranger, a casual human being who took a stroll around Simon's Pool, might think that nothing had happened at all. But much had. And not simply the fact that the water was cleared of all its litter—except for Chester's boat. Simon Turtle was lolling as usual on his log; Walt Water Snake had been swimming and sunning, too—and craning and waiting; the morning seemed perfectly ordinary. It wasn't. There was something in the air. But then, a turtle and a water snake *always* seem to be keeping some secret.

"Not a word, now! At first."

"Don't you be bad, now, Walter," said Simon.

"We have to have some fun! For a while!" And that

human stranger who overheard the two friends talking might have thought Walter's eyes were glinting wickedly. They weren't. It was mischief. However, you have to know a snake well to tell the two apart.

Slipping down and swimming tummy-up—he was expert at different styles, was Walt—the water snake slithered next to Simon and lay on his back, as if he wanted some sun on his stomach. But his eyes were open a little slit, so when Chester appeared: "Good gracious! My word! And upon my soul! Turtle-urtle, we have company!" He zipped over for a closer look. "Chipper Chester—what's *happened?* I never yet have seen a bug with big bags under both his eyes, but if any insect could—"

"Oh, Walter, I'm so tired—"

"Again—?"

"No. Still. I didn't sleep a single wink."

"Hop on the *Becalmed*. I'll rock you."

"I called it the *West Wind*."

"The weather changed. This boat will have a new name every day. Jump! Jump!"

Chester did as he was told. And gratefully collapsed on his ship. "Oh—oh—it feels so good, to lie down." The pleasure of stretching was wonderful. "I just am simply dead."

"Were you up all hours hunting for field mice?"

"I was up all hours—tolling."

"Tolling?" Simon and Walter asked together.

"Chiming!" answered Chester Cricket, with a little bit of crazy impatience. "But of course you don't know —and you wouldn't think it to look at me, would you?—I am a clock now! If you please!"

Simon made a whistling sound—disbelief—as if now he had heard everything. "I have lived in this Meadow since Hedley was only a country village, since before there were houses on Mountain Road, and I *never*—"

Walter Water Snake interrupted him. "How does a cricket become a clock?"

"He tells time," said Chester, matter-of-factly.

"May we hear how this strange change took place?" said Walter. "From cricket to clock? It sounds like a fascinating if somewhat unnatural transformation."

"I have to take a nap," began Chester. "I—"

"Afterwards! Afterwards!" Walt rocked the boat, to prompt the cricket. "You hopped all the way to the Towers Terrific, or Thatchworth Manor, whatever Mrs. Magnificent calls it, and—and—?"

"And all the way there she kept telling me how 'at home' I'd feel. She wanted me not to be disturbed by how 'well off' Jerome and she were. How 'well-to-do.' She said that several times. And she knew that I came from 'modest circumstances.' "

"By which she meant your stump?"

"I guess. You see, she explained, Jerome and she were, well, rather wealthy—"

"Wealthy she said, but rich she meant!" Walter whacked the water with his tail. "Can you beat that bird!"

"It's very curious," Chester reflected. "I thought that was only a human problem. It's one of the big advantages of being an animal: if you decide you're rich, then you are!"

"Yeah, that's probably just how it happened," growled Walter. Beebee Pheasant woke up one morning and said, "Jerome, we are *rich!* Let's add another tuffet, my dear."

"I doubt if she said that," laughed Chester.

"Words to that effect. So what else did Towering Tail Feathers do to make you feel at home? Along with telling you that you were just an impoverished cricket without a hole to call your own?"

"Oh, Walter, it wasn't as bad as that. She was only trying to 'set me at my ease,' she said."

"I'd like to set *her* on her ease!" grumbled Walter.

"Anyway—we got to the Towers, and sure enough, Miss Jenny had wandered away again. But not too far. She was under a patch of daisies, sleeping. So peaceful she looked. And when we woke her up, she said she was hunting for strawberries."

"Strawberries?" said Simon. "In August?"

"When Miss Jenny hunts for strawberries, she hunts for *strawberries!*" Chester said. "She's so old by now that whatever season she wants it to be, why that's the season she's living in. It's wonderful, in a way. And she was absolutely thrilled that I was coming to live with them. She'd been expecting me, she said. I know —don't ask—how could she be? But she was expecting *someone*—that's all—and it might as well be me. You just have to think the way she does—as if thought had all turned into dreams, or memories, or secret desires —and then everything falls in place. And don't you hiss, Mr. Water Snake."

"I was only sighing. It's beautiful."

"I've grown very fond of Miss Jenny, I have! She's a lovely grand old soul! And say what you want about Beebee and Jerry—they love her, too. Although she makes their life a mess."

"Some people—and pheasants—*need* to be messed up!" pronounced Mr. Water Snake, upright as a judge in the water.

"What's strange is, Beatrice said that she and Jerome wouldn't know what to do without Miss Jenny, but now they spend almost all their time taking care of *her*. I guess years ago, when she first came, she waited on them—she got their food, and cleaned the tuffets, and kept all Beatrice's things in order."

"And what," Walter wondered, "did the young Miss Field Mouse get out of all this for herself?"

"Room and board, and security. From some of her rambling last night, I got the idea she was left alone."

"She was. It was terrible!" Simon Turtle remembered. "Her brothers and sisters just up and moved. And Jenny was left alone. Her last brother got killed in a Meadow fire. One horrible, dry August afternoon. Afterwards she was—taken by fright, you might say. She was scary. Can't blame her. It must have been somewhere along about then that she met the Pheasants." The turtle brooded: time worked in his world, which was the Meadow, in strange unforeseeable ways. " 'Course I wouldn't want to gossip, or cast aspersions or anything, but I've always suspected our Beatrice might just want a lady-in-waiting of her own."

A silence lasted and grew so huge it was like a person standing there—some presence that was bigger even than a human being. It made Chester Cricket uneasy. "Well, she's got a fantastic home anyway. You should see all the stuff that the Pheasants have collected!

That's one thing I found out right away—if you're rich, you never throw anything out. And you're very proud of your family, too. Beatrice let me see her eggshells. Of course I wasn't allowed to touch."

"Her own eggshells?" asked Walter.

"She keeps them in a special place. It's a kind of bookcase—except it's for eggs—stitched out of twigs and branches and thatch. She's had several broods, so there's quite a few. There's Betty's eggshell, and James's and John's, Jerome Junior's, Floyd's—I can't even remember. The children are all scattered now. A whole bunch flew to Massachusetts—more room up there. But the queer thing is this: she thinks even more of the 'ancestral eggs' than of her own!"

Walter didn't much like the sound of that. "What are 'ancestral eggs'?"

"They're the eggshells her forebears came out of," said Chester. "All kept in a lunch box she found one day. And is she ever proud of them! The older the better! There's Aunt Helen's eggshell, and great Uncle Ezra's, and Great-great-*great*-grandfather Floyd's—he's the one that Beatrice's fourth son was named for—"

"You've become an expert in pheasant family trees!" said Walter.

"—and Floyd's cousin Alice, twice removed, who

flew west about seventy years ago with her half brother George—and neither of them was ever heard from again—"

"Chester Cricket, you stop that!" Walter lifted his tail, about to spank the surface again.

"All neatly stacked in a dented tin lunch box. Which has the name 'Billy' scratched on it. The really old eggs get yellow, too."

"I think it's creepy!" snorted Walt. "Whoever that kid might be, if Billy should find his lunch box again, he's in for a very peculiar surprise. *Yek!*"

"It takes getting used to," Chester admitted.

"Does Jerome have his own dented lunch box of ancestors, too?"

"No. From hints that Beatrice dropped now and then, I gathered his family wasn't all that distinguished. At least not when compared to hers."

"He could be a peacock—she'd never admit it."

"Oh, and speaking of peacocks—you ought to see all the plumes."

"Whose plumes?"

"Everybody's plumes."

"She has ancestral plumes, too?"

"You bet!" said Chester. "Arranged in a circle, each stuck in the earth, around the central tuffet. Beatrice

calls it 'The Gallery: A Pheasant's Family Album of Feathers.' "

"That does it," said Walter. "I'm going under. Goodbye forever." He sank from sight.

"Walter Water Snake!" Chester pounded the water. "You come back here! You sent me off—at least you can listen."

Walter's eyes appeared and blinked at the cricket. That's all of him he would let be seen.

"Last night, after supper—which Miss Jenny misplaced, but we found it in Sunnyreach—Beatrice pointed out all the colors that came and went in her family feathers. There was one special gold, a bright brown gold, that Floyd the First had—and Beatrice has it, too—"

"Oh, naturally," Walter rose to say.

"—that she thinks is unique. No other pheasant in the whole world has it. She was hoping that one of her children would—but no luck. She has plumes from them, too."

"Does she yank a pin feather before she lets anyone leave the nest?"

"To remember them by. And add to the family album. Tradition. Floyd the First made it a rule: Before any pheasant chick flies away—"

"It sounds to me," Walter interrupted, "as if Tuffet

Towers was haunted by Great-great-*great*-grandfather Floyd."

"Well, it's not," said Chester. "When anybody's as fascinated by ancestors as Beatrice Pheasant is, they don't need any ghosts. They make their own. And why not, say I. Everybody should have an interest. Hers is ancestors, mine is music—as Beatrice kept pointing out when we'd located dinner and eaten it. I didn't know what she was driving at, the way she kept on with the compliments: how 'musical' I was, how 'tuneful,' what pleasure she and Jerome always took in listening to me 'toll the hours.' Do I toll, Simon? I ask you now, do I toll the hours?"

"Not so's I've ever noticed, Chester."

"I chirp, that's all. On nice days I chirp. And on bad days, too, if I feel like it. But Beatrice got it into her head that as long as they had this great big tuffet— the one in the middle, and it was a tower—well, why not make it a bell tower, and why not make me the bell? I just was supposed to hop up there, on top of the tuffet, and strike the hours. And wait, Walter Water Snake! Just you wait—before you start doing somersaults underwater! Not only was I going to count the hours—ring them off all day and all night—she had this little melody that she wanted me to play first. Here, listen." The cricket chirped a simple tune. But it didn't come out exactly right. "No, wait—I'll sing it. I haven't quite got the hang of it yet. It goes: ding dong, ding dong—dong ding, ding dong."

"Why, I know that!" blurted out Simon Turtle. "That's a famous tune for a set of bells. They play it every Sunday morning in that church on Fern Street."

"That's probably where she heard it," said Chester. "And it's very pretty, too. For a church."

"A little grand for a tuffet, you think?" Walt shook his head—and the shake went down all the way to his tail. "I never heard the like of it. Our very own cathedral cricket."

"Ridiculous!" exploded Chester. "Imagine!—me telling the time. I mean, I wouldn't have cared so much, being turned into a cuckoo clock—but a tolling bell is something else. 'Course, never did I dream it would go on all night long. I thought to myself, I'll ding a few ding dongs and put them to sleep and that'll be that. Not a bit of it! Miss Jenny's got insomnia! She sleeps all day and just naps at night. And whenever I was nodding off—the Pheasants were both off in Chillington, where they sleep in the summer, and out like logs as soon as night fell—and just when I was dropping down to a marvelous dark, soft rest myself—which I need so much!—I'd hear this squeaky voice in my dream, 'Chester dear—it's time to

chime!' And all night long! I said, 'Miss Jenny, everybody's asleep. And I don't even *know* what time it is.'
She said, 'Well, you're a cricket, aren't you, dear? And
crickets work by sun and moon and stars, don't they?
And summer and fall and things like that. I thought
all insects had time in their wings.' "

Walter shook his head, impressed and surprised.
"She's got a lot of poetry—for a fuddled field mouse."

"So, just to make the poor soul happy, I'd hop up
on the tuffet and ding some more. Believe me, I
learned to hate that tune!"

"It must be boring," Walter agreed, "to be a clock.
Ding dong, ding dong—and round and round—till
the end of time."

"Toward dawn Miss Jenny nodded off herself. And
she talks in her sleep, too. I heard her mumbling—
why, I think she was saying 'I smell smoke.' " The
cricket's eyes glanced quickly at Simon.

"Ah me, ah me," sighed the turtle sadly. "It well
may be she was saying that. So long ago—yet never
past."

Chester hurried on, "When the sun came up, I
dinged my last ding dong, and came back here. So come
on, Walter—let's hear it."

"Hear what?"

"*Ohhhh—!*" Chester was feeling desperate. His voice

had a reckless note in it—a crazy and gay tone of hopelessness. "I'll start it myself: 'A cricket he lived with an elegant pheasant—' "

"I can't," said Walter, and shook his head. "I'm not that mean. It's sad—sad! *sad!*—the way you get shunted around the Meadow."

Chester Cricket, however, would not be stopped. A fit was upon him; he was hectic and glum, all at once. "Now, what rhymes with 'pheasant'? 'Peasant' does! 'However, she thought he was rather a peasant . . .' I'm sure that Madame Magnificent thinks I am. Or else you could say, 'But life there rapidly grew unpleasant—as he ding-donged merrily!' "

"You are flipping, Chester—"

"I'm not even hopping—"

"You're flipping out! Now simmer down. This isn't the end."

"Oh yes, it is! And I've made up my mind! I'm going over to Mountain Road and let myself be squashed by the very first car that comes along! If I knew how to—and was big enough—I'd eat worms and end it all!"

"I hear some worms are quite tasty," said Walter. "A buzzard once told me—"

"*I don't care what a buzzard told you!*" shrieked Chester. "I have no home! I'm homeless! There's no place in the whole wide world I can call my home! I *am* going to let myself be run over!"

"Why not take a little nap first?" Walt suggested.

"Before ending it all?" The cricket's antennae, which had been stiff and wiggling with rage, began noticeably to droop.

"Sure! Don't you want to look your best? Just lie down there on the—on the"—Walter dunked his head, then lifted it up, like someone's finger testing the weather—"on the *Southerly Breeze,* and rest awhile."

"Well, I—I—"

"Rest!" Walter ordered. Using his chin, he gently forced the cricket down flat. "You rest, Cranky Cricket. Poor cheerless Chester—just rest."

"Oh, all right." Chester heaved a sigh. "Why not? Since all is lost, anyway."

Before the eyes of Walter and Simon, in barely the time that it took for a floating cloud's shadow to pass, he was fast asleep.

"My land!" said the turtle. "I never heard Chester take on like that."

"We got finished just in time," said Walter. He circled Chester, on his boat. "Now, the best way to get him up there is—don't watch this, Simon, you might get the wrong idea." He opened his jaws as wide as he could and took Chester in his mouth. The sight was quite dreadful. A stranger passing by just then would have thought a heartless, hungry snake was about to devour a cricket alive.

TEN

Home!

Home . . .

You always will know it. It may be a mansion on a grand avenue. Or a little bit of shivering nest, where a hummingbird can relax at last. A two-family house—or a two-owl barn. An apartment above a busy street. Or a niche for an insect—just a cell in the bark, and so tiny the tree doesn't know it has guests—but, oh, how it overlooks life, teeming there in the grass! Whatever the nook, niche, or hole may be, the creature that lives there—owl, mouse, or man—will instantly know it: like your fur or your feathers or your own close skin, a home feels only like itself.

Chester Cricket was dreaming that he was at home. There was wood all around him—a round woody shelter was cupping him like a human hand. He was lying on something delightfully soft, and above him hung his bell. It looked so nice and familiar and real that he had to reach up to tap it.

It rang!

Good grass, Chester said to himself. And aloud, "Where am I?"

"You're home!"

The cricket leaped up—scared out of his wits—and, as long as he was in the air, wheeled around and came down facing opposite. Two grins were beaming in on him. Bright sky was outside. "Walter—Simon—what happened?"

"Har har!" Walter laughed—real laughter, too; no sarcasm now, so very pleased with himself he was, and with Chester and the world. "We fooled you—"

"You should've seen us working!" said Simon. "All yesterday and—"

"But we did it! Oh, yes! We—"

"Boats, indeed! I never made boats in all my life."

"But I don't understand," began Chester. "How—"

"Everyone's talking at once," said Walter. "Why don't all turtles and crickets relax? Just sit back and collect their breaths. *I'll* explain! Well, now"—he cleared his throat—"it's been grand fun for everyone —except you—to watch the crinkly cricket here go moping around our beloved Old Meadow in search of a place to lay down his head. Alas, with little success,

Home!

I fear. He's been kept awake, made to wash his feet, and been ding-donged half to death. But enough of sorrow! Away all woe! Begone, all ruthless misery! The hour of joy at last is here! It's *time to chime!*—as someone once said. Cheerful Chester now has his home at last! He is in residence! Har! har!"

With a whoop and a holler, Walt's head disappeared. Chester hopped to the opening and looked out. He realized he was up toward the end of Simon's log, the highest part, at the end of the crack where he'd slept the first night. Below him—the pool; above him—the sky; around him—the rich living afternoon. "I don't remember a hole here," he said.

"There wasn't one," said Simon, who was lying just outside. "I gnawed it out myself!"

"You *gnawed* it?"

"You never saw such chewing!" called Walter. "Turtle-urtle and I decided that if he could gnaw you out of one house, why then he could gnaw you into another. So now you have a home designed by me and built by the Simon Turtle Construction Company." Like a quick black rope, he whipped himself up beside Chester. "He got splinters, too, but with these fabulous fangs of mine—which work like surgical instruments —I painlessly extracted them."

"And if you'll notice"—Simon pointed out a special

detail—"I made the hole a little bit higher than this crack. That way the rainwater'll all run off." He was very proud of his architecture. "I'd really like to have chewed two rooms, but I couldn't get my head in that far. We can hire some termites, if you wish to expand."

"And *I*," said Walter, "while you were asleep, I slithered over to Littleville and talked the two titanic chipmunks out of a choice fern mattress for you. And Uncle was glad to spare a thorn, to pin up your bell."

Chester Cricket was—"Overwhelmed," he murmured. "I'm just dumbfounded."

"You think you'll be happy here? Do you? Huh?" Walter thrashed with a kind of glad impatience. "With Simon and me? Underneath the Turtles and Serpents Monument?"

"What monument?" laughed Chester.

"We haven't put it up yet," said Walt. "It's going to be Simon, reared up on his sturdy hind legs, with me balancing on the tip of his nose." He leaned toward Chester and slyly confided, "We're both reptiles, you know. Although I'm more 'rep' and Simon's more 'tile,' as you see from his beautiful slate back."

"We'd love to have you here, Chester," said Simon.

Walter Water Snake lifted threateningly. "And I'll bite anybody you want me to."

Home!

"Oh, Walter," said Chester, "you've never bitten a soul, and you know it!"

"It's true." Shamefaced, Walter hung his head. "Not a single bite." Then lifted it quickly. "But I've hissed at millions! I *am* a—well, you know—a snake, remember. And I do not like to be plagued or pestered! My reputation will keep strangers away. So all our guests will be welcome—or else! But that's not the point, ol' pal, ol' buddy, ol' Chester friend!" Walter wriggled all over the end of the log. There are times when hands are especially helpful: to wring, when you're worried. "The point is—can you be *happy* here? You're a persnickety kind of a crickety, and—and—"

Chester did not speak a word. He hopped to the very top of the log. Before him, like ruffled blue glass, was the pool. And behind, on the opposite side, he could see where the brook made a sudden turn. The current there quickened—the surface sparkled like shattered silver. Simon's Pool always caught the sun.

"You know," mused the cricket, "this spot reminds me of my old stump. The brook turned there, too. I used to like to watch the water. As a matter of fact—and I've never told this to anyone—I had a secret name for my house."

Chester Cricket's New Home

"What—?"

"What—?"

"Brookview. In my heart, I just thought of my home as a place where I could see the brook."

"Well, you can here, too!" burst out Walter. "And it even can have the same name—"

"No. No." Chester shook his head. "Each home should have its own name. A *good* home deserves to keep its name, squashed or whole." He shielded his eyes from the light with one foot. "If I lived here—if I lived here—I would call this home Turnbrook. It's like, but it's unlike, my stump, both at once."

"I love it! I love it!" said Walter. "Turnbrook. *Turnbrook!* How distinguished! How right! How like the choice of a critical cricket! Both modest and appropriate. Do stay, Choosy Chester! Just think of the fun we can have! We'll go boating, exploring—we'll make music together!"

Then all at once, for no reason at all—except the best, pure happiness—Chester Cricket began to laugh. "I'll stay." His heart shifted into a new position. "I'm going to love it here!"

"Hoo-*ray!*" Like a singing black arrow, Walter flew through the air. *"Ohhhh—"*

He rose from the surface and finished his song:

Chester Cricket's New Home

A cricket lives beside a brook—
In Turnbrook House lives he!
He has a new home now—and look!
He has a new friend—ME!

It was late in an August afternoon, but the world felt deep and tall and wide. It felt—as it always should —like new.